Sorry, Not Sorry

LINTUSEN PRESS
PRESENTS

Sorry, Not Sorry

An unapologetic celebration
of Canadian life through story

LINTUSEN
PRESS

On the Trail of a Canadian Hero

SHIRLEE SMITH MATHESON

I had long been seeking a Canadian hero, to feature in a story or perhaps even as a basis for song lyrics. The United States has many. We constantly hear their songs of worship and learn of their contributions to American history, sports and culture, but Canadian heroes seem all too rare. We know they must be here, coexisting with the general populace, but how does one find such a creature?

By plotting basic human needs and habits, it became evident that tracking a hero would be similar to tracking a forest animal. They all must drink. As most naturalists simply establish themselves at likely-looking watering holes and wait, I decided to employ the same tactics.

The nearest watering hole to my domain was the one and only local hotel. Its bar was a noisy cavern decorated with objects indigenous to the area: dog sled runners, bear and beaver traps, crosscut saws, double-bit axes (secured to the wall), and the horns and skull of a mountain sheep, complete with eye sockets enhanced by blue lightbulbs. The ceiling was lined with flattened egg cartons to help absorb the noise. The wood floor endured much abuse from scraping chairs, muddy work-boots, spilled beer, and detritus of empty potato chips bags and peanut shells. The tables were stacked with beer glasses, and plates containing the remains of hotdogs and pickled eggs, and a centre pile of cash in readiness to pay for further rounds.

This was the environment I chose as the most likely for finding a Canadian hero.

By pursuing my research with the diligence and hope of a novice anthropologist, I soon became established as a fairly regular member of the society that came to drink at twilight. As the regular inhabitants became familiar with my scent, they no longer shied away when I approached them, although I could see they were at once alert and curious as to my purpose. Thus, I spent the greater part of one winter and the following spring on my field surveys.

Had I been using traps to catch my specimen, I would have inadvertently caught many innocent and unwanted types, for during the first months of my sojourn I seemed to attract everything but heroes. In Canada, and especially in the North, a splendid variety of creatures are forced to share the same watering holes. This being the only one within a forty-mile vicinity, it was indeed a focal point. Down they came at dusk: some furtively, hesitantly, casting their eyes right and left as they quickly opened the double doors and slunk into the noisy and darkened interior. Others advanced boldly, befitting such kings and queens of the forest. Still others came toting their mates, sipping for a predetermined time, and then leaving as shadows lengthened and the more voracious of the species emerged.

Quietly I sat, listening, watching, and waiting for that special example. How does one recognize a species never before captured in Western Canada? On I listened, measuring my own liquid intake to not cloud my perception, until finally, in May, on a Friday nearing midnight, I bagged and tagged a hero.

His camouflage was excellent: shaggy hair and unshaven face; a solid build, stocky and bearlike, not fleet but strong and heavy – a startling creature who, I learned, was sometimes given to over-excesses at the watering hole. Although his temper was quick and his habits bordering on bizarre, he was basically a fine animal, of pleasant nature when not riled. I had come to know about him through his constant patronage at my stakeout, and had been amused to learn of his unorthodox reputation as a gourmet cook. "You've never tasted a better beaver or lynx roast, stuffed with wild rice, than one Jim McEvoy has had his hand in. He just works magic with 'em," one local inhabitant informed me. "Can that guy cook!"

That particular Friday evening I had greeted him automatically while keeping my eye on the crowd. He sat down at my table and our conversation began with casual and common inquiries: "Where are you working now, Jim?" I asked, knowing he had been unemployed for part of the past winter.

"Chetwynd," he grunted, his head bobbing at each word. "Crane operator. Swinging pipe."

"That's a long way to drive—forty miles each way."

"That's all right. Don't want to work for the Yanks on the dam. Hate Yanks."

"Why is that?" I asked, although it was not an uncommon statement around here. An American corporation was one of the main contractors for powerhouse construction on the hydro-electric dam being built here on the Peace River.

"Always hated 'em," Jim replied. "Hated 'em in Korea. Know what they had us doing over there? Shooting Americans. Canadian shooting Americans, in a war that wasn't a war, in Korea. Beat that, will you."

"How did that come about?"

"Well," he said settling his body back into his chair and his mind back to December 1952, "I was enlisted in the 11th Airborne Division, Royal Canadian Regiment. We were in a place they called 'The Hook'. The Canadians had gained some territory, pushed ahead, and the Yank troops were told to hold the position. Then up comes Colonel Peter Bingham, says to me, 'Sergeant, just got orders from the company commander—we've got to form a line back here and shoot every Yank that retreats.'

"We had to form a back-up line to shoot Americans that retreated from the front!"

"Was that common—Americans retreating?"

He gave me a scathing look. "Yep," he said. "Was."

"So, the Americans had the North Koreans shooting at them from the front and the Canadians from the back if they retreated?"

"Yep. Kind of caught in the bite, eh?"

"Any of them retreat?"

"No, thank God. They didn't that time. Stupid Yanks, giving us orders like that! Canadian shooting Americans." He shook his head, a man who had been there, and who carried firsthand knowledge of American wartime buffoonery.

"Well, that's pretty sad," I acknowledged, and then added, "but you can't judge all the people of the nation by one commander's orders. There are lots of heroes in the United States, too. We hear of them all the time. In fact, you almost have to be a States-side hero before you're considered one in Canada."

He sank back in his chair, head slumped toward his barrel chest, his beer glass nearly hidden in his large paw-like hand. He surveyed the dissipating foam on his beer and scowled into the recesses of the glass. Suddenly his grizzled head jerked up, black eyes swung toward me, through me. "I'm a hero in Canada," he said.

I went wild, nearly scaring off my specimen.

"A hero in Canada," I repeated softly, as I considered slipping a tether around his foot to hold him. A hero in Canada. "What do you have to prove it?"

"Medals."

"What kind of medals?"

"Life-saving. Saved a kid from drowning in Wabigoon Lake back in Ontario, 1959."

After serving two years in Korea, Sergeant James Alfred McEvoy had completed his military service in Ontario as instructor of Small Firearms. And it was here that the lifesaving incident occurred. He smiled, happier now, recalling an endeavor of greater value than standing in line waiting to shoot retreating Americans for the American government.

"I had to dive into eighteen feet of water," he continued. "Brought him up and used a Holger-Nielsen method, you know, with arms. The kid was down ten minutes. No one thought he'd live, but he did. No brain damage either. He's still living today.

"I've got them at home somewhere. Nice medals, too. Medal of Honour from the Queen, the other from St. John Ambulance. But, they had to chase me seven years to give them to me. Couldn't find me."

We talked a few more minutes, with Jim revealing he'd been born in Mine Centre, Ontario, on August 5, 1930, and had received his schooling in Fort Frances. He'd then ventured west to Vancouver Island and worked in the logging industry for MacMillan Bloedel, until enlisting in the army. In 1964, he'd moved to Hudson's Hope BC, where I'd found him. As a member of Local 115 Operating Engineers, he'd worked as a heavy equipment operator on local projects and pipelines. But now most of the local projects were completed, and so he'd found work in the nearby town of Chetwynd. But, my mind was no longer on the topic of his current livelihood: I had found a Canadian hero.

He left me then, to join his friends at a nearby table while I pondered what he had told me. I overheard his conversation, now on subjects of more immediate importance: the log house he was putting up this summer, and predictions of the moose population this coming fall.

Canadian heroes don't linger much on past glories, I

mused. And, poets don't labour over sagas praising their deeds, nor historians painstakingly gather their data for annals of history; schoolchildren aren't asked to memorize songs extoling their glory. But how great, I wondered, was the distance between an anthropologist's endeavor to seek out a particular person or species, and those of the lyricist who makes up rhymes and ballads to preserve the memory of such people and bring their deeds to the consciousness of the public? It shouldn't be too difficult to think up a melody and a few lines of verse about my discovery.

Let's see...hmmm, hmmm, hmmmm... That's it! Now, let's try this:

I was looking for a hero, trying to find the man
who could represent Canada, show them where we stand.
I looked in Parliament, and I looked in the schools
but the farther I looked the more I found fools, till I found...
Big Jim McEvoy, drinking in the bar.
Tell them Jim McEvoy, tell them what you are!"

Note 1: James Alfred McEvoy was killed October 2, 1978, the day after he read and approved a draft of this story. It was subsequently read at his funeral by the minister in St. Peter's Church in Hudson's Hope BC. My husband William was one of the pallbearers.

Note 2: *Alaska Highway News,* August 20, 1984,:

"Local Family to Sue Ford".

Wanda McEvoy, widow of James McEvoy who was killed when his 1978 Ford F-150 pickup jumped into reverse and rolled over him near Hudson's hope BC on October 2, 1978, is now suing Ford for damages. McEvoy's lawyer is claiming that Ford was negligent in not designing this particular model of vehicle so the automatic transmission could not accidentally slip into Reverse from Park, and further neglected its duty in not informing owners of this danger. No dollar figure for the claim has been stated.

Note 3: See Google: Ford Transmission Failure to Hold in Park – The Centre for Auto Safety

Shirlee Smith Matheson's literary career has offered her invitational visits to numerous schools, libraries and museums throughout Canada. Research introduced her to a variety of characters featured in her 21 published books, and short stories and articles. Shirlee has served on multiple occasions as a writing instructor. manuscript evaluator and writer in residence. Website: www.ssmatheson.ca.

The Day My Aunt Florence Rode an Elevator With Gordie Howe

CHRIS MCMAHEN

I think the only reason my Aunt Florence invited me over for supper every Saturday night was to watch Hockey Night in Canada with her while Uncle Clyde worked on his miniature train set in the basement. I'd eat my tuna noodle casserole off of a flimsy aluminum T.V. table while she would shout at the T.V., especially when the team she loved with all her heart, the Detroit Red Wings, was playing.

But Saturday nights with Aunt Florence were never quite the same after Tuesday, June 18th, 1974. That's the day my aunt had a near death experience which involved her Bible, an elevator, and hockey legend Gordie Howe.

At 1:55 p.m., my aunt pressed the button for the elevator in the lobby of the Eden Gardens Apartments on her way to her weekly Bible study group in Mrs. Burke's apartment on the fifth floor. When the door opened, Aunt Florence stepped into the elevator. But unlike the dozens of rides she'd taken previously in this elevator, this particular time, Aunt Florence felt as if she had stepped into an alternate reality where she didn't quite belong—an alternate reality where Detroit Red Wings hockey legend Gordie Howe rides in an elevator.

Even without his Detroit Red Wings sweater or the number nine on his back, Aunt Florence knew it was Gordie Howe. Even through the snowstorm of T.V. reception that was lousy no matter how much Clyde fiddled with the rabbit ears, she knew exactly what he looked like. And there was no doubt this was Gordie Howe. He did, admittedly, look shorter in real life, but then he wasn't wearing skates, so that would account for a few inches.

Even though this was Gordie Howe, Aunt Florence felt compelled to adhere to a strict code of conduct of appropriate behaviour when a single woman rides in an elevator unaccompanied and in the presence of a man who is unknown to her. Stand with your back against the wall furthest from the man. Clutch your Bible tightly to your chest. Keep your eyes focused upon the floor. Stand still. Don't utter a word. Endure.

While she managed to uphold her high standards of decorum inside the elevator, my aunt felt like she was immersed in an atmosphere of the ethereal. This was a circumstance above and beyond her earthly expectations.

Aunt Florence had experienced her fair share of unanticipated twists of fate in her long life. Her brother, Alvin, running off with Reverend Smart's wife—she never saw that coming. And winning the meat draw down at the Legion eighteen years ago came out of nowhere. To any unexpected incident that fell into Aunt Florence's straight and narrow path through life, she would say, "That's life for you."

But this was different. Nowhere in the script of my aunt's life was there a scene where it was written, "Ride in an elevator with Gordie Howe." This was beyond being merely unanticipated. This was unearthly.

Until this moment, Gordie Howe was a tiny black and white character skating across her ten inch T.V. screen on Saturday nights. Or he was a grainy photo in a newspaper. Gordie Howe wasn't supposed to be riding an elevator at the Eden Gardens Apartments on a Tuesday afternoon. Only mere mortals did that.

"There's an explanation for everything that happens in our lives," my aunt would wax philosophically, usually after her third sherry before dinner at my parents' house on Sundays. But this extraordinary circumstance—Gordie Howe in an elevator—had pushed her powers of explanation to their outer limits. "For me to share an elevator with Gordie Howe could only mean one thing," my aunt said. "I must have died suddenly, and I was on my way up to Heaven escorted by Gordie Howe."

Accepting her fate, my aunt wondered about the circumstances of her sudden, expected death. Was she hit by a bus after stepping off the sidewalk to cross Market Avenue? Did she get electrocuted when she pushed the button for the elevator? The possibilities were endless, but ultimately the outcome was all that really mattered. Maybe God was softening the blow of her unexpected death by having her ride up to Heaven with Gordie Howe.

Did this mean that Gordie Howe had died, as well? Imagine the coincidence. Or maybe in the off-season, he just worked for God. After all, everyone knew he was more than a mere mortal. Whatever the case, riding with Gordie Howe in the elevator to Heaven took a bit of the sting out of dying before her neighbour, Esther Simpson.

"She always had her eye on Clyde, and I had no doubt she'd be moving in for the kill as soon as I was out of the way. But then, why should I be worried about earthly matters when I was riding up to Heaven with Gordie Howe?"

As the elevator rose, Gordie Howe finally spoke to her: "What floor do you want?"

My aunt lifted her eyes from the floor, glanced his way, and said, "Just press the button for the Pearly Gates."

And so, my aunt soaked up the moment, enjoying this once-in-an-eternity experience of ascending to Heaven in an Otis elevator accompanied by Gordie Howe.

During the ride, she couldn't help but reflect upon some regrets. There was that second honeymoon to Niagara Falls she and Clyde never made. And she never did get to hear Neil Sedaka sing "Calendar Girl" in person.

Although my aunt was somewhat disappointed to have her life cut short at the tender age of seventy-nine, her first impression of the after-life was pretty good, especially if this elevator ride was a taste of things to come. Gordie Howe in an elevator, then what? William Shatner as her hairdresser? Stompin' Tom as a waiter in the dining hall?

All too soon, the elevator paused.

The door slid open, and my aunt had her first glimpse of

Heaven. She'd done plenty of imagining over the years as to what Heaven would look like. She envisioned a bright immaculate place, with pretty much everything a variation of white.

But her first glimpse of Heaven through the open elevator door was of a dimly lit hallway with a stained red carpet, an artificial rubber plant, and a velvet painting of a matador hanging crookedly on a wall.

This couldn't be the right floor. Maybe the elevator had to stop in Hell on the way up. Or maybe this was Purgatory, because it sure didn't seem like Heaven.

And then, Gordie Howe did the unthinkable. He smiled, nodded, and stepped out through the open door.

This wasn't right.

Gordie Howe was supposed to escort her to Heaven, whatever floor that was.

What was going on here? Where was he going? My aunt's mind flailed about, trying to make sense of it all before Gordie Howe disappeared into eternity.

"Wait!" my aunt shouted.

Gordie Howe paused out in the hallway. As the door began to close, she could think only of one way to hold him.

"Can I get your autograph?"

Gordie Howe held out his arm, the door halted and obediently re-opened.

"An autograph? Sure," Gordie Howe replied. He pulled a pen from his pocket and clicked the button on the end with his thumb in anticipation of being handed a piece of paper to sign.

My aunt now faced another crisis. She never brought her

purse on the bus with her to the Bible study group what with all of those purse snatchers. The only thing she had was her Bible.

Aunt Florence could think of no alternative. As the door began to close, she held out her Bible, and Gordie Howe took it from her hand just before the door closed.

She frantically pressed the Open Door button, and a few seconds later, it opened. The hallway was empty. Gordie Howe had vanished.

But there, on the carpet just beyond the open door, was her Bible. Aunt Florence stepped out of the elevator, picked her Bible up off the floor, and opened the cover. On the first page was scrawled, "Best Wishes, Gordie Howe."

My aunt heard someone call her name from down the hall. It was Mrs. Burke, standing at her open apartment door. "Right on time, as usual," she said.

Every year, on June 18th, my aunt brings out her Bible, opens the cover, and points to Gordie Howe's autograph. Then, she always says to whoever will listen, "You know, the French may have their Joan of Arc, and the Irish their Saint Patrick. But we here in Canada have Gordie Howe. Larger than life, but not too large to ride in an elevator.

Chris McMahen is the author of four books for young readers. Box of Shocks *won the* Manitoba Young Readers' Choice Award, *while* Buddy Concrackle's Amazing Adventure, Klutzhood, *and* Tabloidology *were selected "My Choice" by the Canadian Children's Book Centre. He is a past winner of the Okanagan Short Story and Word on the Lake writing contests. Chris has also written for local theatre groups and published sleep-inducing academic papers. He currently lives in Salmon Arm, British Columbia.*

Cold Masks

Marc Watson

There was a sound in the open space as the blades cut through the frozen surface like a whetstone passing over a chef's knife, smooth and harsh at the same time.

That feeling crept in as the world was obstructed and obscured by the cage on his face. His heart was, paradoxically, both full and empty. Hockey was Tyson's only solace in a world that had moved past him too quickly.

The ice was pristine. A rarity on these local rinks. Some old rat in the maintenance shed cared when they set the levels on the cleaning machine. Someone had really taken their time, trying to capture pure Canadiana. It was likely that people who came here all the time, or worse only once or twice a season, didn't know how good they had it.

The ice wasn't full, but more than a few of the younger faces looked up and beamed as he strode confidently across the rink. He could hear the wind in his ears and feel the bite of the season on his cheeks. Was this heaven? If you caught it in just the right light, he was hard pressed to tell otherwise.

The first excited shouts sounded off as he took his place at the lonely end of the rink. It takes a special kind of person to willfully abuse themselves the way he did. Make no mistake, it was absolutely abuse. But for Tyson, it was also therapy, and was far more helpful than lying on a faux-leather chaise and talking about the mixed emotions he had about the things his father had done to him in the guise of trying to make twenty thousand people chant his name.

"Goalie!" came a voice from beyond the well-beaten boards, scarred with decades of puck marks and physical contact. Goalies were rare on small town rinks. All of those with that gift in their youth had either moved away to ply their trade with bigger clubs, or aged themselves out of an activity that wasn't practical anymore. Kids had long ago mastered the ringing clang that echoed through the spruce trees nearby as they shot another off the posts, but there was a special exhilaration that only came from putting one past an actual defender of the iron cage.

He nodded to the humble crowd to indicate that he was ready, and the first young face rushed at him and tried to sneak one between his bulky, well-aged, pads. They had likely seen more rubber than the nearby highway. Worn, but not useless. Not yet.

Tyson wasn't sure when it happened. He wasn't paying attention when the world faded away. Clarity hit his system like a drug. The anxiety the world tried to crush him with was held at bay. The cold, sure truth of the mind behind the battered mask echoed: stop the puck.

He had gotten hooked on this feeling when he was a kid. It was so simple when he was younger. Fresh leather and pine sap and the acrid aroma of brewing coffee swirled around him when he opened his first pair of pads on a cold Christmas morning.

Now there was only the cold, and the truth: stop the puck.

They had their tricks. They always did. Those country boys who hadn't stopped trying to hide their disappointment that the scouts weren't going to call, spun and cut at angles that made their parents' bodies ache to watch. Their legs twisted and bent like corn stalks in the wind, but all for nothing as the puck hit his blocker, or had the satisfying clap as it slunk into the back of his glove.

The adults were smarter, but no more successful. They had the power that their progeny lacked. They would move slowly and reel back the canon while for one brief moment when they flexed and pushed, their ages left them, and they were children again playing at the game they loved. The slaps were deafening, and more than one could move the vulcanized rubber with an audible hum. Still, they couldn't beat him.

Stop the puck.

He wasn't completely unfeeling. He knew the unwritten rules. He would always let the youngest of the crowd, those that were maybe on skates for the first time, shuffle forward and emulate their heroes. Tyson would feign effort and dive like a caricature, allowing the barely-touched puck to trickle past his reach and cross the invisible line. Their smiles were priceless as they tried to celebrate their victories, only to end up falling. They didn't care. Parents cheered and older siblings scowled. The sound of their happiness was magnified by the Canadian cold.

He caught sight of the girl across the ice. She was dwarfed by the caged backstop behind the opposing net. She stood watching, with her legs covered by ripped street hockey pads that weren't fit for ice and would likely do more harm than good if she ever took a shot worth stopping. She had a blocker made of something resembling little more than cardboard, and a baseball glove for a trap. An oversized player helmet and cage on a head covered with mousy brown hair. She had nothing else to protect herself.

Tyson saw shadows of himself in another time. Her eyes were focused on him. He knew that look. He knew those eyes.

It wasn't a need to show off that drove him. He was not so vain. There wasn't a person on the ice that could beat him without cheating or trickery. That was a fact, not a boast. He had an audience now. He had a fan. He was a hero, and heroes show you what is possible within yourself. Suddenly, the murky shadow of the former glory chased actually dispersed. This was what his father had never understood: Tyson had never wanted twenty thousand voices screaming his name. He'd only needed one set of eyes that actually cared about the art he was trying to perfect.

It was now showtime for the only audience he cared about: the kindred spirit two hundred feet away.

The players lined up and tried their damnedest once more. Tyson felt his body clench and loosen with their movements as they cut the white surface like raked grass. Twisting backhands sailed wide and booming slappers only prairie boys with an ocean of bailed hay behind them could muster thudded off his pads like dead meat. He took the shots. He stopped every one.

By now it was a challenge. This stranger had to be beaten. There had to be a way, and each player believed they knew how to do it. They would have known their best chance was a two-man rush, but there was no sport in that. This was one on one, skill against skill.

This was Canada, in the heart of the flat land and rusted combines, and this was how Canadians took their rank.

In his mind, there were only the mechanics and the Zen. An amalgamation of physical engineering and spiritual release. It was an addiction, and it was medicine. A twisted version of mental health therapy. His muscles closed and stretched, a coiled snake on the frozen water.

The young eyes of the opposing goalie watched from a distance. Then she skated slowly. Found her place, her home in front of the far net.

While a shooter spun and danced toward her, she moved with him, mimicking Tyson's silent and stalwart figure in the distance.

At Tyson's end, one young man with a stick that likely cost more than all the gear Tyson had on his body came close, fooling him on a right shot backhand, only to slip it between his legs and deftly handle the puck to the fore. Tyson had to split and stretch, growing larger with each moment, until the toe of his pads caught the rubber and drove it wide. Hollers from the gathering crowd as each thought their compatriot had succeeded. But it was just another whiff, and so, it was just another failure.

The girl in the far crease aped the move, impressing Tyson with her flexibility and determination. This one has it, he thought. This one has the curse.

Wagers were made now. Beers for the seasoned crowd, and Cokes for the younger. Tyson wasn't a fool. It would be beers all around, regardless of age. There were no rules out here in the wide-open.

They thought they'd fool him. One father blasted him, missed, and then wrangled his puck on the rebound. He took up a perch next to the net, trying to carry on a conversation to distract the newcomer from what was likely his son who was coming next. "Where ya from?" he asked.

Tyson was amenable enough. "Highcross, out east," he answered. He knew the type. The guy wasn't about to dig out his cell phone and look it up, only to realize there was no such place. He likely didn't have his phone on him anyway. This was father and son time, and in places like this that kind of thing was important. Borderline religious.

"Oh yeah, oh yeah," the man shot back. Feigning interest. Faking knowledge. He thought the quick motion he made with his hand was missed, telling the next in line to go. Thought he was clever, despite having digits like a bear paw inside his glove.

The younger face coming at Tyson was a dead ringer for the rough and weathered older man beside him. This was Canada, in the heartAll a good bit of fun the years in the Change Room Club snapping towels and hurling insults bought you a lifetime membership to. After all, if this stranger wanted to come to their rink and try to run the table on them, it was already *game on*.

The younger half of the subterfuge charged forward while the older struck up again. "You guys had good weather out that way? Looks like we're about to get another blast of winter before the day is out, if those clouds up north have a say." Clever. Tyson almost respected the attempt.

"Oh Lord, no," he replied, holding his place, the middle of his chest constantly aligned with the movement of the puck while he watched the young man's core muscles give away his next move. "Cold. Damn cold. Had to fire up the generator..." a flashy stick save sent the puck careening off into the corners, shattering the deception "...a few times because the lines froze. Haven't seen it this bad in years."

Downtrodden with the failed attempt, father and son skated off without another word said.

Behind the puck-marked goalie mask that rattled like old car parts when hit, Tyson was a monk. He smiled and he gabbed at times, but with each shot he was freed from the concerns that had brought him here. Fishermen found their peace on the water. Tyson found it in a goalie crease.

Down the ice some of the fresh younger ones had begun shooting on the girl. One shot lifted and she took it off an unpadded shoulder. Concern washed over Tyson as he felt the sting empathically, until she deftly cleared the rebound.

He took a stinger off the back of his leg on a shot from a big guy with an aged Budweiser toque. It snapped him into the moment just as he was sure the high shot down the ice had done to his compatriot. They were of a breed that only really felt pain in the locker room, but that didn't mean they weren't reminded it existed every now and then.

Damn, that one hurt. Or at least it would. Right now, the

next player in line was already on the rush, smelling the blood in the water. There was no time to dwell on the pain. That was the life of a netminder. If a Centre on the backcheck took a blast to the ankle they could skate to the bench. Maybe they miss a shift. Take one like that while you were in net and it meant that you left a fat rebound in the open ice. There was no room for mistakes. No time for discomfort.

His save wowed the crowd. More than one of them began to see the moment for what it was. Something different, in a place where different didn't always play nicely. Different often meant government regulations and tragic back road accidents. Long droughts or longer rains. 'Different' was a reason to get your back up.

This time, different was beautiful. It made their world larger in all the right ways. Here, on their humble rink, was a solidification of their belief that hard work could pay off.

To Tyson, the adrenaline rush consumed. He chased it to small town rinks like this just to get through the day. This was the price an adrenaline junkie had to pay, and the desperation didn't always feel like a reward.

The morning carried on and the faces began to vanish. Tyson's blissful headspace began to recede. The hardest part of being an addict is the realization that the drug isn't enough anymore, and all good things must end. It will make you feel like a god. Then it will kill you.

Highs like this, even 'natural' ones, were no different.

How long had passed? An hour? A year? Did it matter? The drench of salty sweat on his brow told the story. Too long. Time to pack it in. The thought of leaving the ice made depression hang over him like a noose as he stood one last time and gave a wave. The show was over. The curtain was drawn. A fist bump or pad slap as he left the company of the die-hards still skating in the chill with nowhere better to be.

How long ago did the young girl leave? He'd lost track. Felt stupid. Stupid for wordlessly connecting with her. Stupid for cheering for her. Stupid for missing her exit. For all his sense that she was the most important person on the ice today, he hadn't noticed when she'd left.

A warm blast from the off-ice change room of the old barn welcomed his body as the aches and pains began to announce themselves.

Thankfully, the young goalie was there, her father nearby, checking his phone as she finished packing her bedraggled gear in an old duffle bag, her wet hair tied back in a loose ponytail. How old was she? Ten? Eleven? Just a pup. He'd never been that young. He'd stake his life on that fact.

"Oh hey!" said the father, tucking his phone away. "Great job out there, man. You really put on a show." Was he one of the shooters?

"Thanks. It was a lot of fun," Tyson replied, trying to seem normal. Trying to act like he wasn't the saddest man in the world. This was as close to a championship dog pile as he got these days, a post-shinny praise and a hearty 'good job'. If he was lucky, someone might buy him a Tims.

All things considered, that was probably just as good.

Tyson took off his mask. The dad smiled, as if something was given away. Tyson undid his pads. Tried to ignore the possibilities.

"I thought so," the man said.

Tyson was made.

The man's phone came out again. He held it out, encouraging Tyson to look up. Forcing him. Trapping him in the moment. "That's you, yeah?"

Tyson looked, unable to avoid the question.

There it was. That face. The face he'd worn like a mask for most of his life. Smiling. Youthful. Fake as a three-dollar bill. "It was, once," Tyson answered. Tried to sound aloof. Tried not to sound disrespectful or weird. Wasn't sure he succeeded. Didn't care.

"Wow, geez kid. What are you doing here? Aren't you supposed to be up with one of the big clubs by now?"

Ha. Not likely. He never wanted the glory. He only wanted the feeling.

For years he'd convinced himself that he needed to be the best. He was convinced that to get that rush, it was only available with success and cold clarity the goalpost gateway offered him. The higher he went, the greater the feeling would be. He was wrong. His father was wrong. He could get it anywhere. The demons were worse the higher you climbed. Why would he want to fight where the air was so thin? He got as much of a rush on the rinks and ponds of backwoods farming towns, with fewer things that made him seize up inside. He had realized too late he could get the joy without the anxiety. His father had never forgiven him.

"Nah," Tyson replied. Figured a half-truth beat a total lie. "I wasn't cut out for it." Considered saying more. Realized he didn't need to. That pretty much summed it up.

The dad put the phone away into over-tight jeans. "Well, I guess I'll never know. You sure worked us over, though." A nod of appreciation. "It was good for her." He indicated the girl, blushing and shying away. "She's wanted to be a goalie since the day she could walk."

Tyson looked down the bench, trying not to seem intimidating. He knew that feeling. Knew that drive. "Is that true?"

Nothing at first, then a quiet voice. "Yeah. I like goalie."

Tyson smiled. Sized up the father again. Would he push her? Would he say and do the things his father did? For better or worse? "Yeah. I like goalie too." Winked at the dad as they shared a wide smile.

Silence for a moment. Tyson started stripping his sweaty gear, damp and hot.

"Jeez, kid," said the father, "you look like the northern lights."

Damn. Gave more away. Stole a glance at himself and saw his ribs and legs. Purple, blue, red, and some colours even God didn't know were invented yet. The cost of the position. The street price of the adrenaline he needed to get by.

"Well, it's what I pay I guess. No helping it."

"Is that why you quit? Get hurt?" the dad asked. He seemed genuinely curious.

If Tyson had to guess, he'd say there was a measure of concern there for his daughter. Was this what she would pay too? They both hoped not. Her hopes were a mystery.

Tyson nodded. "Something like that, yeah. It's sure not for everyone." That was the truth. No lie needed.

The daughter finished getting changed and her fourth-hand gear was tucked away. Her father leaned over and said something to her as he shouldered her bag. Likely the abbreviated backstory of Tyson Houlihan. His entire life summed up in a ten second whisper. Then they walked over. The father shook his hand and thanked him for coming out and giving the locals something to talk about. His hand was hard. Calloused and strong. The currency of the land was how tough your hands were. This man was well paid. The daughter said nothing. Contemplating something. A million complicated thoughts in a face so young.

Before they left, she turned back. "Dad says I can play next fall. Or maybe just get some better gear."

A non-committal face from the father.

Tyson knew all about the things we tell our children. "You should. I was watching you out there. You've got what it takes." He didn't care if the father approved. He had let her start the conversation, after all.

"If I come through again, I hope I get to see you play."

"The boys laugh. There are no girl goalies around."

Tyson nodded. Hockey and misogyny were as intertwined as goal net mesh. "It's hard. Trust me, I know. Boys or girls, it doesn't matter. It's hard." He stood, his still youthful body cracking more than it should. "It's good for your head, though." Could something be a total lie and the complete truth at the same time?

The dad's eyes softened. Smart people out here on the backroads. Ones that know a moment when it's happening. "Any tips for her?" he asked.

A lifetime of them. Only one mattered. He looked down at her, trying to make his dark eyes show her how important the words were. "An army of people will tell you it's too hard. They may throw numbers and videos at you, or insults and bad words, but they're all just going to make you stronger, and get you to the same goal. There's really only one goal. Stop the puck."

She smiled, a dimple forming above the end of her lip. "What if I don't?"

Tyson shrugged, the weight of the world nowhere to be found. "Then you just have to stop the next one."

She considered that for a moment, but the deep thoughts weren't done yet. "Do you really like it? Being a goalie?"

It was Tyson's turn to smile. That was the question he'd asked himself every day of his life. A question with only one answer. "It sucks."

A wash of dejection on her face. She didn't get it. Not yet.

"Hey,"

She looked up at him again.

"I like it because it sucks."

Even if it was as faint as a firefly, a light dawned in her eyes.

Both men knew that was going to be enough, and her dad ushered her out the door.

It was silent in the changeroom as Tyson watched her climb into the front of her father's truck and pull away. He finished packing up, not caring in the slightest that he may have sounded like a weathered old man dispensing platitudes with the things he said to her. He was an expert on what this ice could do to a person. Truth be told, he was likely the utmost authority.

There was an actual, genuine smile on his face as he walked back out into the early afternoon chill. Nothing was left but the creak of the building sway, the drone of the ancient heaters, and the dim buzz of the omnipresent fluorescent lights.

__Marc Watson__ is a genre-fiction writer of all lengths and styles. Hailing from Calgary, Alberta, he has five published novels, and a number of short stories in various anthologies. When not writing, he's often found on the ball diamond, cooking for his family, or judgmentally eating poutine.
marcawwatson@gmail.com

Redcoats!

SEAN DONAGHUE-JOHNSTON

*""I saw a man come from the fence, when I said to my comrade
'There is a man, I'll have a shot at him.' Just as I had said these words
and pulled my trigger, I received a ball under my left ear, and fell
immediately; in falling I cut my comrade's leg with my bayonet. He
exclaimed 'Byfield is dead'—to which I replied—'I believe I be,' and I
thought to myself 'Is this death, or how men do die?'"
Shadrach Byfield, Battle of Frenchtown, War of 1812*

Colin McIntosh adjusted the flint on his musket for the
sixth time in the last thirty minutes. He pinched the
sharp stone between thumb and forefinger and
wiggled it to make sure that it was snug, then loosened the
screw and started over.

"You're going to shatter that flint, son," Skip Govern said.
"You don't want to overtighten it."

"I know," Colin said. "That's why I'm trying to adjust it."

"Want a hand?"

"No, thanks. I think I got it now."

Colin finished tightening the screw, then leaned his musket against a tree and rested his elbows on his crossed legs. He looked at Skip and smiled. Skip nodded, put his pipe in his mouth, and turned toward Neil Hood, a retired history teacher from Chatham, who was in the middle of a story.

"So they amputate his arm," Neil was saying. "And after the operation, he asks an orderly, 'What did you do with the arm?' And the orderly says, "What arm? Oh, right, that arm. We threw it in the dung heap out back.' So he's about ready to punch the orderly in the face, except he remembers he doesn't have a fist to punch with. It's out back in the dung heap."

Colin laughed with the other Redcoats, who were sitting on logs or on the ground with their backs against trees, their faces turned toward Neil.

"Is that Shadrach Byfield you're talking about?" Skip said.

"That's right," Neil said. "The indestructible Shadrach Byfield, Pierre Berton calls him, on account of him surviving just about every battle up and down this border."

Skip nodded and smoked his pipe.

"So anyway," Neil continued, "Shadrach digs his amputated arm out of the dung heap and he gives it a good cleaning—you know, to get all the dung off it. Then he gets someone to bang together a tiny coffin, and he gives his arm the military funeral it deserves. After that, his stump heals, and he's back to playing cards with his fellow soldiers for a quart of rum."

Colin smiled and ran his fingers over his slick forehead and through his damp hair. Then he unbuttoned his wool coat, unzipped the nylon pouch that was strapped against his stomach, and pulled out his cell phone.

Swapnil Kumar, who had been striding by with his bicorn under his arm, stopped and said, "What is that contraption, private?"

Colin looked up at the gold lace and buttons of Swapnil's uniform. Swapnil was in his mid-thirties, which made him a teenager compared to most of the other men here. And if Swapnil was a teenager, Colin was a baby.

"Hi, Dr. Kumar," Colin said as he tucked the phone back into its pouch and buttoned his coat. "I was just checking the time, sir."

"Isn't that what pocket watches are for?" Swapnil said. Then he raised his voice so that the others could hear him. "We'll be getting into formation in half an hour. Listen for the bugle. The siege will begin at exactly two."

"Yes, sir," some of the Redcoats said. Others merely grunted.

"Many of you will be killed in action," Swapnil added. "And if you get yourself killed, please be good enough to stay dead until the end of siege. Your king and country thank you for your sacrifice."

Swapnil looked at Colin and winked. Then he turned on his heels and strode toward a group of green-coated Loyalists who were on the grass playing frisbee.

"Anyway," Neil said to those who were still listening, "Shadrach goes back to England, where he used to be a weaver, and he realizes that he won't be able to support his family anymore, because who ever heard of a one-handed weaver? But then one night he goes to sleep and he has a dream about a loom that can be operated with one hand. When he wakes up, he sketches the design on a piece of paper, and he brings the sketch to a blacksmith, and the blacksmith makes it for him. And he spends the rest of his life providing for his family as a dreamweaver. Get it? A dreamweaver."

"Ha," a few of the Redcoats said without conviction. Most of them had begun checking their powder and collecting their gear. Some wandered to the edge of the woods to urinate, while others walked back to camp to use the Johnny-on-the-spot.

Colin picked up his musket and fiddled with the flint.

"Ready, son?" Skip said to him.

"I guess so."

"Thought about when you're going to die?"

"Not really. I mean, I guess I've been wondering when the best time would be."

"Want my advice?"

"Sure."

Skip puffed on his pipe a few times, then said, "Well, you don't want to die too early, because then you miss the whole battle without firing hardly any shots. But you don't want to die too late either. Everyone likes to die at the end of the battle, which means it gets awfully crowded up close to the fort. And, if you can help it, make sure you're far away from the crowd when you fall, because the kids like to throw pebbles at the dead soldiers. Best thing to do.... What's funny?"

Colin was smiling, thinking about the time he and his brother had thrown not pebbles but popcorn at one of the dead soldiers. "Bugger off!" the dead man had barked, and they ran away laughing.

"Nothing," he said to Skip. "Go on."

Skip grimaced and rubbed his chest.

"*Ogh*," he said.

"You okay?" Colin said.

"Heartburn." Skip explained. Then he cleared his throat and continued: "Best thing to do, in my opinion, is to find a nice comfy patch of grass right in the middle of the battlefield, where the dead aren't all lying on top of one another. If there's a tree with a bit of shade under it, so much the better. But that'll be prime real estate. Hard to get."

"Comfy patch of grass; shade, if possible. Got it. Thanks, Skip."

"Don't mention it."

A Canadian militiaman was walking from the camp toward their group, carrying a musket. Despite the mustache and the green uniform, Colin could tell that it was Keely. The stiff wool could not completely conceal her curves or the fluid switch of her hips, and she was wearing her aviator sunglasses. Her strawberry-blonde hair was tied up under her military cap.

As Keely approached the group, one of the old-timers whistled. Keely gave him the middle finger, and the Redcoats laughed. Keely smiled.

She walked over to where Colin was sitting, put her free hand on her hip, and said, "Hey."

Colin used his musket to pull himself up, and they stood facing each other.

"Hey," he said.

"Like my mustache?"

"It suits you."

She smiled, and Colin flushed, sure that he'd said the wrong thing.

"Hey, you two soldiers over there!" one of the old-timers called. "I don't know what you're up to, but whatever it is, I'm pretty sure the military would have frowned upon it in eighteen-fourteen!"

"Don't ask, don't tell," Keely said over her shoulder, and the Redcoats exploded in laughter. She turned back to Colin, stroked her black stick-on mustache, and said, "I've been looking for you."

"You have?"

"Yeah. My father wants to talk to you before the siege starts."

Patrick Bodkin was inside one of the white tents, propped against a card table and talking to Orillia Roy. He was dressed, Colin knew, as Sir George Prevost, governor-in-chief of British North America during the War of 1812. His scarlet tunic was decorated with an elaborate webwork of gold braids, and his black bicorn, which he held under his left arm, was enormous.

Orillia sat cross-legged on a folding chair, a pad of paper in her hand and a pen between her teeth. She was wearing jean shorts and a Lowest of the Low t-shirt. Colin stared at her for a moment, then looked down at the ground. The last time he remembered seeing her was when he'd tried to work up the courage to ask her to prom and ended up vomiting on her shoes.

"You've seen the turnout," Patrick was saying to Orillia. "The numbers aren't in yet, but all signs suggest that this will be the biggest reenactment in this town's history."

"Biggest in what sense?"

"Biggest in every sense: crowd size, number of participants, explosions, everything!"

Colin stood by the entrance, holding his military cap in one hand and his musket in the other. Keely sauntered to a chair and sat down on it with a clatter of buckles.

"Ah, here's my daughter again," Patrick said. "And she's brought Private McIntosh back with her. Hello, Colin."

"Hello, Professor Bodkin."

"Colin is one of my honours students," he explained to Orillia. "I've managed to coerce him into participating in the reenactment. For extra credit, of course." He gave Colin a wink.

"Hi, Colin," Orillia said.

Colin blushed and said, "Hi, Orillia."

"Oh, you two know each other!" Patrick said.

Orillia drew her feet under her chair and grinned at Colin. "We go way back," she said.

Still holding his musket, Colin wiped sweat from his brow with the back of his hand. He looked at Keely, who was still wearing her aviators. She seemed to be watching Orillia, but for all Colin could tell she may have been asleep. He looked at Orillia and wondered how she knew Professor Bodkin. Then he remembered.

"Oh, you write for the *Chronicle*," he said.

"I don't just write for it," Orillia said. "I *am* the *Chronicle*. There's, like, zero staff other than me."

"Oh," Colin said. He tried to think of something else to say, but nothing came to mind, so he just turned red.

Keely yawned.

"Mademoiselle Roy is covering the reenactment," Patrick explained. "And I figured she'd like to get another young person's perspective."

"Oh," Colin said again. He looked at Orillia, who raised her eyebrows and held her pen at the ready. "But...we're supposed to be getting into formation soon."

"This won't take long," Orillia said. "Just a few questions so I can get a quotation or two for the article."

"Okay."

"First, why don't you tell me about how you got involved in the reenactment? In your own words."

"Well, that was thanks to Professor Bodkin. I'm a history

major at Drummond University, and Professor Bodkin is my advisor. He has a big collection of War of 1812 stuff, and he has some uniforms and muskets. He asked me if I wanted to participate in the Bicentennial, and I said yes. So he lent me one of his uniforms, and he helped me get my black powder musket training, and...um...that's about it."

"Is that how you became interested in the War of 1812?" Orillia said. "Or were you always interested in local history?"

"Well...I grew up here...as you know...so I've sort of always been surrounded by it. My friends and I used to sneak into the old fort and play war. When we were kids, I mean."

"So you've always been interested in the War of 1812," Orillia said. "Has the Bicentennial helped to intensify that interest at all?"

Colin looked from Orillia to Patrick, who was watching him eagerly.

"Um..."

The bugle sounded, followed by the collective rattle of soldiers preparing for battle. Colin looked at the tent flap, then back at Patrick.

"Ignore it," Patrick said with a wave of his hand. "Go ahead and answer the question, Colin. That's an order from your governor-in-chief."

"Okay...um...what was the question again?"

"How has the Bicentennial intensified your interest in the War of 1812?" Orillia repeated.

Keely cocked her head and watched Colin from behind her mirrored aviators. All three faces—Orillia's with the pen between her teeth, Patrick's with a nod of encouragement, and Keely's with what appeared to be a smirk forming at the corners of her mouth—were turned toward him.

Colin wiped sweat from his upper lip and tried to think of something to say. Something quotable. But his mind was blank.

"Colin," Patrick said. "Didn't you say something to me about how the Bicentennial events have really brought the War of 1812 to life?"

"Oh, right," Colin said.

Patrick nodded and extended his palm toward Colin, as though he were passing something to him.

"The Bicentennial events have really brought the War of 1812 to life," Colin repeated.

As Orillia scribbled in her notebook, a light, metallic jangle came from the side of the tent where Keely was seated. Keely was holding her fist against her mouth and her shoulders were shaking with suppressed laughter.

"Thanks, everyone," Orillia said, getting up and heading for the exit. "I'm off to find a good spot to watch the battle. Give 'em hell, Colin."

"You too—I mean, good seeing you."

When Orillia was gone, Colin turned to Patrick and said, "Sorry, I couldn't think of anything to say. I guess I got nervous."

"No!" Keely said with a cackle and a snort. She got up from her chair, slapped Colin on the shoulder, and moved toward the exit.

Patrick smiled and put his hand on Colin's shoulder. "You did just fine, private. Now get out there and take that fort."

Soldiers in British and Loyalist uniforms were ranked shoulder to shoulder across the freshly-mowed battlefield. They were flanked by a patch of woods on the right and an audience on the left. Straight ahead was the American-held fort, grey and brooding, with a Star-Spangled Banner rustling in the cool breeze overhead.

"'We few, we happy few, we band of brothers!'" Neil Hood bellowed. "'For he today that sheds his blood with me shall be my brother!'"

"Who invited Shakespeare?" someone chirped, and a ripple of laughter made its way down the line.

"I'll be damned if we didn't get the worst spot," Skip muttered as he rubbed his chest and eyed the boys and girls pressing against the wooden barrier. "Watch out for pebbles," he reminded Colin.

An old-timer behind him snorted and said, "Tell the little bastards they'd better watch out for my bayonet."

"Do not bayonet any kids, Jughead," Neil Hood said, "or you won't be invited back next year."

"Bugger that!" Jughead said. "What kind of war are they running here anyway?"

Colin leaned forward and looked down the line to where he could see the green-coated Loyalists positioning themselves on the opposite flank. Beyond them he could see some of the First Nations warriors, their position along the edge of the woods hinting at greater numbers hidden among the trees.

When he turned back, Skip was flashing his dentures at him.

"Who's the lucky lady?" he said. "You two an item?"

"No," Colin said. "We're just...." He shrugged, and his red, sunburned cheeks became redder.

"Why don't you ask her out on a date?"

"I don't know," Colin said. "I guess it's because I get nervous."

"That's no reason," Skip said. "Everyone gets nervous before doing a thing that's worth doing. Then they do the thing. Or they don't."

"Yeah, I guess."

Skip gestured toward the battlefield. "Lots of kids your age and younger fought and died here on this battlefield two hundred years ago," he said. "I wonder how many of them got killed before ever working up the courage to ask out their sweethearts."

"Sweethearts?" Colin said, smiling.

"'Theirs not to make reply,'" Neil Hood belted out from behind them, "'theirs not to reason why, theirs but to do and die!'"

"Shut it, ya numpty!" someone said in a fake Scottish accent.

"*Ogh*," Skip said. "Who's got Rolaids?"

Swapnil Kumar, who had been in conference with his

fellow officers, broke from the knot of gold-buttoned uniforms, took his place near the end of the line, drew his sabre, and called out, "At–TEN–*SHUN!*"

A clatter rolled through the line, then tapered into a taut silence. A series of orders were given, the fife and drums and bagpipes started to play, and the Redcoats began to move as one. Far across the battlefield, before the stout grey walls of the fort, Colin could see the waiting blue line of the American infantry. A hush fell over the crowd.

For a while, nothing happened. The British, Canadian, and Indigenous forces moved slowly across the field, measuring their steps to the beat of the drum. Then cannonfire flashed from the bastions of the fort, the sound of thunder rolled over the open field, and dirt was flung up into the air where charges had been buried by explosive technicians earlier that day. The audience applauded, and the soldiers continued their slow march toward the fort.

"*Ogh,*" Skip said, scratching his chest.

More cannonfire, and soldiers began to fall. Colin squinted as bits of dirt from one of the blasts pelted his face.

"Whoa, that was close," someone said. "Anyone else think that one was a bit close?"

"They trying to kill us?" someone else said.

"You know," Neil Hood said from over Colin's shoulder, "if this were a real battle, the cannonballs would rip right through our lines and there would be a pink mist over the battlefield."

"Pink?" Colin said.

"That's right, a pink mist of blood."

"Quit scaring the kid already," Jughead said. "Anyway, it's the grapeshot you really gotta worry about. Tear you to bloody ribbons."

They were getting closer to the fort. Colin could now make out the faces of some of the American infantrymen. One grizzled old man with a Civil War mustache seemed to be staring right at him.

The Americans lowered their muskets, took aim, and fired. Swapnil barked orders, and the Redcoats responded in kind. The sound of musketfire crackled across the battlefield. When Colin fired, he aimed for the grizzled old man, who seemed to be aiming at him.

The two armies exchanged volleys, back and forth, back and forth. *Make ready! Present! Fire! Load!* Again, and again, and again. Men were dropping like flies. Colin was locked in mortal combat with the grizzled American, who never seemed to take his eyes off him. *Make ready! Present! Fire! Load!*

Slashes of smoke were drawn in the air by musketfire, then smudged by the breeze. It got smokier with each volley, so that it was through a haze that Colin saw his rival fall.

"Gotcha!" he said beaming, and he turned to Skip.

But Skip was no longer standing beside him. He was on the ground, lying on top of his musket.

Colin waited for the next American volley, then joined his friend on the grass.

"You bastards!" Neil Hood shouted as he fell. "He was

just a kid!"

Swapnil gave the order to fix bayonets. The Redcoats shouted three *huzzahs*, then charged the American lines. Colin remained perfectly still as they stepped over and around him. He lay there for a while, listening to the clash of bayonets and breathing in the aromas of mowed grass and gunpowder. Tiny insects bumped against his lips and eyelids. Eventually, he crooked his head and rested his chin on his forearm so that he could watch the action: the Americans retreating, the British pursuing, the scaling of the walls of the fort. He could almost feel the audience holding its breath as the siege rushed toward its climax. Then he felt a hard tap on his shoulder. He turned toward Skip, but Skip was still lying on his musket, his face turned away.

"Hey, Skip," he said. "Good show, eh?"

Colin flinched suddenly as a small object sailed through the air, bounced off his arm, and settled in the grass. He lifted himself on his elbow to see what the object was—a peanut, it turned out to be—and, as he did so, he was struck again, this time on the forehead.

"Ow! Hey!" he shouted at a pack of sniggering boys and girls, who responded with a renewed barrage of peanuts before being chased off by good citizen-spectators.

Colin smiled and turned again to Skip, who was unchanged, except that there was a peanut resting in the cup of his ear.

Staring at the peanut, Colin said, "Skip?" He touched Skip's shoulder and said again, "Skip?"

An ant crawled across Skip's temple, but Skip himself did not move.

"Skip!"

Suddenly, an explosion rocked the battlefield and an orange-yellow fireball appeared over the fort. The audience gasped, then applauded. This was the grand finale, a pyrotechnic simulation of the moment when, two hundred years ago, a powder magazine ignited and two hundred and fifty lives—British, Canadian, Indigenous, and American— were lost in the resulting explosion. As Colin rolled Skip onto his back and shook his shoulders, the audience's attention was fixed on the column of greasy black smoke that was now rising from the fort.

"Help!" Colin shouted. "Someone! I need a doctor here!"

"Look!" some of the audience members said, and they pointed at the Redcoats who were dropping like smoked hornets from the walls of the fort. "Ooh!"

"Help!" Colin shouted again, but his cries were lost in the fog of simulated war.

People stood around in loosely knotted groups, speaking to one another in hushed voices. Some watched silently with crossed arms or hands over mouths. The siege having ended, red and green coats now mingled with blue, war bonnets with baseball caps and sunhats, officers with privates, soldiers with civilians.

Colin sat on the curb at the edge of the parking lot. Someone had led him there and sat him down, but he could not remember who.

He was able to catch bits and pieces of conversations that were going on around him.

"Tragic," one woman said. "Just tragic."

"I wonder how long he was lying there before someone noticed," another said.

"Is he dead?" a child's voice asked. "Mommy? Mommy? Is the man dead?"

"Heart attack, is what I heard," a man said.

"I just hope it doesn't overshadow an otherwise—you must admit—very successful reenactment." This last voice Colin recognized as belonging to Patrick Bodkin. "Still, devastating, devastating."

Patrick was speaking to Orillia Roy, who glanced over at Colin, then looked quickly back at Patrick.

Colin realized that someone in a green uniform had walked up to him and was now standing over him.

"Hey," he heard Keely say.

"Hey," Colin said without looking up.

"Bummer, eh?"

"Yeah."

"Honestly, though," Keely said, "I'm surprised this kind of thing doesn't happen more often. Half of these guys look like they could keel over any second. I mean, look at that guy. He must be about a hundred."

Colin looked up and saw that Keely was referring to the grizzled American, who was standing near the playground, leaning heavily on his musket. Colin and his former rival made eye contact and exchanged solemn nods.

"PRESENT ARMS!" Swapnil's voice boomed suddenly from somewhere in the crowd.

Colin leaped to his feet and held his musket vertically in front of him. Other soldiers, regardless of rank or allegiance, did the same. Those who did not have their muskets ready to hand saluted. Audience members and other civilians removed their hats and bowed their heads. The bagpiper played "Going Home" as paramedics wheeled the bodybag past the saluting soldiers and loaded it into the back of an ambulance.

After the ambulance had driven away, Colin turned to face Keely. He remembered what Skip had said to him on the battlefield: *Everyone gets nervous before doing a thing that's worth doing. Then they do the thing. Or they don't.* It was time for Colin to do the thing. Except, he realized, he was no longer nervous. Maybe he had conquered his fear. Or maybe he was in shock. Or maybe...maybe the thing wasn't worth doing after all. The things that he had feared—rejection, humiliation, failure—suddenly didn't seem so bad.

Colin looked down and shook his head.

"Sorry, Skip," he said under his breath.

"What?" Keely said. "Did you say something?"

"No," Colin said. "Nevermind."

Keely shrugged and wandered over to her father, who had just concluded his interview with Orillia.

Orillia walked away from Patrick, past Keely, and up to Colin.

"Sorry about your friend," she said.

"Thanks," Colin said.

"If you'd like to say some words about him for the *Chronicle*, let me know. But not right now. I came over here as a friend, not as a reporter."

She gave him a hug, then stepped back and smiled at him. Colin smiled back. Looking at her now, he remembered how much he'd liked her in high school, how much he regretted never asking her out. He opened his mouth to speak, then suddenly put his hand over his mouth and said, "*Glulch*."

Orillia moved back instinctively. "Colin?" she said. "Are you okay?"

Colin swallowed and took a deep breath. "Yes," he said, "I am now."

Orillia laughed nervously and gave him a sidelong look. "You're not going to puke on me again, are you?"

"I might," he said. "But before I do, I need to ask you something." He looked out toward the battlefield, then back at Orillia. "Would you like to go out on a date with me some time?"

Orillia looked at Colin for what felt like an eternity. Her eyes squinted, the corners of her mouth lifted slightly, and her nose twitched.

Colin prepared for the worst.

"Yes," she said after a while. "Yes, I'll go out on a date with you."

"Really?" Colin said. "I mean, that's great!"

"Let me see your phone."

Colin dug his cell phone out of its nylon pouch and handed it to Orillia, who punched her number into it.

"You still owe me a pair of shoes, by the way," she said. Then she hugged him and left.

Colin was beaming when Neil Hood approached him, put his hand on his shoulder, and said, "We lost a good one today, but we also gained a good one. I wish I had a good quote for you, but I've already used the only two I know. What do you want from me, I'm a history teacher, not an English teacher. See you next year, kid."

Without waiting for a response, he slapped Colin on the shoulder and left him standing there, still beaming.

Sean Donaghue-Johnston is a Niagara-based writer and a professor of philosophy. His fiction has appeared in Space Squid, Broken Pencil, *and elsewhere. He is currently working on his first novel.*

Tofino

NICK PERRY

When Roberta was small, she was indiscriminate from the other children in her town. She wasn't the largest, nor the oldest, and, in any school photo from her primary years, she blended in amidst the forest of oversmiling faces. Her classmates assumed she, like them, had a predominantly Indigenous heritage. She did as well, based on her reflection. That was until a brief project into the history of her family revealed the origins of her hair and skin colour were actually Spanish. It was a strange discovery since no one in her family spoke Spanish and the west coast of Vancouver Island was about as far from Spanish shores as one could get. No one in town seemed to mind and these facts didn't do much to change how Roberta thought of herself.

School passed by and Roberta was a fine enough student across her subjects with the outlying exception being music. There she not only showed a clear ability to take in new knowledge but to extend beyond the boundaries of beauty showed by her teachers. Songs had been part of her upbringing, so much so that her parents couldn't remember if she learned first to speak or to sing. Her teachers, her experts, sat astonished at this young person and the wonderful sounds she could create.

As she played more into maturity, more of Roberta's peers began to notice her talents. They, of course, were not merely talents. More of a mixture of upbringing, honing, failing, and persevering. To the world outside, however, it looked as though the notes and tunes left her as easily as her breath. And they were beautiful songs. Even if she sometimes drifted towards melancholic melodies, they rarely left the listeners in a state of isolation. Rather, they could recognize and relate their own feelings to the song and feel a greater connection to something they couldn't grasp but could feel passing over them. The storms and sunshine were equally sought after. She would play her songs to the other students in her class, then to her grade, and, eventually, for the entire school. It was scarcely populated but the resulting enthused reaction brought up in Roberta a keen sense of joy. Especially since, as a rule, she never performed covers—even when her repertoire was slim. It was sometimes a pressure when the audience would call out for something familiar, something they could sing along to. But Roberta believed in her small catalogue of songs and, if necessary, would play repeatedly until the crowd learned the words.

When she finished school, she did her best to make her living as a musician. Nothing else seemed natural, no other interpellation called her name. It would be difficult, she assumed, but her mother had told her that beautiful things are sticky and if what she was doing was truly beautiful then people would stick to her music forever.

At first, the people who came to see the shows were only those that had grown up around her. There was little avenue for newcomers but this was fine by Roberta. Each show felt like something of a tied bond briefly uniting the members of the public and the art of her playing. She allowed herself to write songs with only the local audience in mind to references of a life only they would understand. Night upon night, they sang the comforting melody of "The Schooner," ingested the full complexity of "Wolf in the Fog," and had their fun clapping along with "Shelter and Shed." Her songs were still stunning in a way that made the listeners forget about envy as each new song radiated like another day of summer.

It had taken years but, with dedication, Roberta had built up enough of a crowd to be sustainable. The winters were harder as there wasn't as much of a pull for live music. With a strong summer, she could persevere through the thinner times. While she would sometimes have to take the occasional job at the grocery store or the pharmacy, she couldn't give up on her music. Each night, once the sky sprinkled itself with stars, she allowed her nature to blossom out through her instruments. Roberta was establishing a life based on who she was and that was its own gratification.

After one particularly shining summer, Roberta's mother sent her a clipping from a national magazine. In the years since high school, she had been releasing her songs to little success online with the most common critique being that the songs, while enjoyable to listen to, were incomparable to the live show. The particular beauty of her voice needed to be felt in behind the breast and not only through the ears. Since she lacked the kind of recording technology of the pros, and so clearly seemed stuck to her part of the world, the best way to feel her revelation would have to come through travel. In so many words, this was the central tenet of the newspaper critic's review.

A chain of lost sources tugged him to one of her shows. Arriving in the crowd unnoticed, he snuck to the back of the room after being cautiously eyed by the locals. His pale skin and sharp sports jacket made him a standout in a town of toilers. He was polite and deferential and by the end of the show he had been utterly charmed by the sweetness of the songs. When it came time to report, he found himself remembering to be a writer first and a critic second. Leaving the snarky cleverness of his profession, he broke through to sincere poetry in his praise. Not only was it impactful to him personally, as her mother had circled, but this review had been picked up by several major news and music publications across the continent.

In a moment of disconnected unity, people were swept up in the words of a stranger and sought out this music that was, supposedly, so transformative. Like seals at dusk, each of these people, in their own way, began to pop out at the sound of her voice. There they spun and noticed another side of the world, an inviting side that they could perhaps be made welcome. After that review, if the planet could have hummed, it would.

By the time the next summer came, Roberta was no longer touring in coffee houses or local halls but larger theatres just outside of her town. It was local enough to still feel familiar but the distance felt like a noticeable change. Once the seating of these venues hit their regular capacity, the number of nights extended to the point that even the weeknight shows were sold out.

Each night brought in a different tide of people and when she had fleeting interactions with these concert-goers, they appeared as people first but then as questions. Questions like: how did a couple from Montréal or Brazil or even Liechtenstein not only hear about her but make the decision to travel? They must have saved money, booked off work, gotten advice from friends, and traversed a distance longer than Roberta had ever known, just to try and capture happiness in her presence. She wanted to sit with people like this, to learn about their lives, but they were all in for the same outcome: to hear her songs, take their pictures, and leave her, too caught up in their own memories.

After a few summers, it was clear that the local venues were not enough to hold the crowd. A few investors had heard the shows and insisted on planting their money in the town to build hotels and halls in a more contemporary style around the town. While the idea of touring was discussed, Roberta became queasy about leaving her land behind and felt it better that the songs were performed where they were written. The money backed her up on this since staying put wouldn't cost anything and there were plenty of places to stay. But there was still the issue of capacity. By now, shows were jammed with people each bobbing their heads amongst the others for a glimpse of a clear view. The owners of the venues worked together on a solution. It was they who landed on where the world would fit: the beach. The decision was presented to Roberta without her input and, as the plans were already beginning, her role was to politely say yes and act like it was her wish.

In a way, it was her wish. The songs were like a turtle's eggs to her. They were delicate and did not respond well to mass changes in environment. But when they hatched, they scattered and sought to find their essences far from their origin. As much as she wished she could have held on to her eggs, kept them buried in the common sand of her home, she had to relinquish her hold on their nature and let them swim or drown.

The date of the beach show was set for the August long weekend. The promoters of the event decided to do away with limits on capacity and allow anyone with the money to pay to claim a spot. This decision trickled into a flood as the influx of people buying tickets manifested itself in cramped roads into the town, overcrowded hotels, fights between families about lateness, and the excessive pollution of transportation, driving either much too fast in a display of excitement or dangerously slow as the drivers were hunched over the steering wheels looking for directions in a town with few signs. Despite their various intents, the tourists settled themselves into their first evening, the first sunset of their vacation, anticipating the consonant sounds to come.

On the night of the show, Roberta moved languidly to the centre position of the westward facing stage.

The crowd crammed together into such a large mass that they covered every grain of sand and, even murmuring, drowned out the ocean. It took them a moment to notice the reason for their evening on the stage. When they did, they opened up with the sound of the sun and rumbled like so much passing thunder.

Roberta gulped at the sight of the scene. Until now, she had not been one for stage fright as the performance of her music was as instinctual as blinking. But against the mass before her, the brightness of the low sun, and through the wonderings of how they would hear, she felt the heavy tug of being overwhelmed.

She dared not to speak to the crowd as it would have been impossible to create the kinds of intimacy she had been used to. So she began to play. Her voice held strong through the beginning but, once the crowd caught on the words and joined in, it became their show.

The screams of approval from them were so loud that they filled the air to the point where there was no room left for Roberta's music. They would chant and cry out, remaining silent only long enough to recognize what was next, before tossing themselves headfirst and without consideration into the tune. After she had played through her setlist and politely waved her way off the stage, the crowd demanded more. More songs, more music, more senses, more enjoyment. Even though they had been the dominating force of the evening, and Roberta's repertoire was still not huge, they expressed themselves as mob to hear more.

Roberta stood backstage, holding her guitar tightly, and faced her body entirely to the east. The rightful darkness of the night was curving up the altering sky as she swayed between her options.

She could give in to them, sing popular songs and discard

the discipline of her artistry to only sing what she had written. Or she could play the same songs again and risk this fickle crowd turning on her, exposing her lack of options. Her thoughts flittered as she wished for the ability to quit. But she couldn't. She had dedicated too much of life to her music and removing that would be like removing her skin. There was no other work for a lifelong artist anyway, no transferable skills, nothing for a resumé. The reactions to her music were ruining her. They had been ruining her for the last few years without notice and what now felt like barbs had presented as bumps in the past.

By its beauty and its attractiveness, her music was pulling in a larger tide than its wharf could hold. Its popularity, which she may have claimed as a goal in her younger days, was swallowing her passion with self-manufactured glee. Standing offstage, with the waves of voices crashing beyond the curtain, Roberta feared what might be done to her if she hid. She faced back as the sun was falling below the horizon in an explosion of red, orange, and pink and did what her spirit required of her. She played on as the crowd demanded, feeling somehow stuck in their desires.

The next day, the beach was a scattered wreck of plastic, alcohol, clothes, and glass, corrupting the sand's pure beige blending to the blue sea. The crowd had been fulfilled on their terms, most never having heard of Roberta in her quieter days. They abandoned the town and the music with a significant trace, nearly all of them scheming as to when they would return to hear her next. Traditions were being established, rooms were being booked, and more good times were being anticipated. As the extra exhaust from their vehicles puffed a last stain of smoke behind them, they smiled through their ignorance. They had been made happy and would do anything to live that feeling again.

The people of the town poked out of their homes like moles. Everyone but them was gone and as they reclaimed their streets, everything felt smaller, slower. They should have been glad but after having held the prosperity of that weekend, enough of their hearts turned to wonder what it would take to be that busy all the time.

Roberta hadn't been seen in days. She resided in her home, the home she afforded with her songs, and avoided work. The excess of people and light had drained her of all will and impulse to create, insisting she rest. It was an insistence that emerged every time she picked up her guitar. Even if she merely wanted to play, the touch was off. For so long the instrument had felt as warm as flesh under her fingers but as she slid her pads over their strings, the biting and sawing steel was uncomfortable. Not that the guitar was much use to her as the port that harboured her creative wishes rocked uneasily.

After a few weeks of nothing, she took a walk down to the beach where she had played the large concert. By now the wind and water had pulled away all the debris and scent left by the audience until there was no conceivable trace anywhere. Long, decrepit logs lined the sand with a collection of empty shells scattered along every step. It was evening and the clouds that hung over the horizon were in motion. Roberta took a seat on one of the logs and looked out into the ocean. Overhead, an eagle soared from a tree. Straight and true, its unbeaten wings carried it nearer to the horizon.

Winds blew against it, forcing it to hover without hurry, until new gusts caught its feathers and propelled it on. She watched as the white of its head and brown of its body were overcome by one smooth silhouette as the clouds opened enough to reveal the setting sun.

The limitless nature of the skyline opened its chest to the fullest expression of the night's takeover. All the waters burned with gold, mauve, and cinnabar. It was becoming too bright to see the eagle yet Roberta strained against the light. Its flight was unencumbered as its shape was swallowed by the ever-changing, never-satisfied mass of the sun.

In that moment, she called out, praying that the eagle would divert itself and return to the trees that had nestled it. But it was impossible for the trajectory it had set for itself was too easily swept away by the invisible beauty of the world.

As she watched the eagle disappear, a recognizable inkling sprouted. At first, her blood ran with excitement only to congeal, questioning both its purpose and its future. In her head was a new song.

Nick Perry is a classic combination of schoolteacher and writer. His debut novel, Broken Water, is available everywhere through Chicken House Press. He's happy to call Port Moody home.

Skates and Dreams

MATTHEW HENEGHAN

eneath a chilled February sky, I joined a nation in watching with bated breath as our boys took to the ice to play a storied game that was shaped by the frozen lands we call home. The red of their jerseys symbolizes far more than just our national flag, but also the blood that pumps in each of our veins. Hockey. Whether you're a fan, a player, or both, or even neither, the significance of this game is tethered to our identity.

At its core, it's just a game. A pastime. Though woven in its evolution, it has become something so much more. Gold medal games tied to Olympic glory. National rivalries. Talking points around the water cooler at work. An eleven-year-old boy holding a branch shaped like a hockey stick slides his feet along a patch of ice etched to the face of the lake. Steady like a fawn. Speaking to himself excitedly as he nears the imaginary net—he shoots, he scores! In his tiny jubilant mind, the crowd goes wild. He wins it all. The big game. The timeless moment.

When his mind returns to his body, he understands the crowd isn't really a crowd at all. It's just the wind playing on the barren branches of winter trees. He stands alone on the lake wondering hopelessly what it would be like to skate like they do. His heroes.

Trevor Linden. Pavel Bure. Mike Modano. The great one.

For years he begged his mother. Not every day, all day, mind you. There were days where she was just too sick. Cancer. On those days . . . the bad ones . . . he'd simply sit next to her hospital bed. Occasionally tossing glances out the window overlooking McGuire Lake. He'd watch as neighbourhood boys and girls moved like poetry on ice. Effortless glides followed by skillful stops and turns. It's a mesmerizing game. Hypnotic in its pace.

When this boy turned thirteen, he was at church one evening in the late summer. The tips of the leaves on the trees beginning to show signs of cooler weather to come. A kind figure came to him and said that the church would love to help him reach his goal—they had generously paid for his registration and donated some money to his mother so that she could purchase some second-hand equipment. The boy's ears pulled back with disbelief and glee. He was going to be a hockey player!

While all this was going on, the boy's mother was a province away in Calgary receiving specialized treatment. One evening she called home to inform him that she had gotten him a helmet and some skates. An immovable grin stapled itself to the boy's face. It was all finally coming to reality.

As is the case with reality, many times it rarely lives up to the dreams we conjure. The boy's mother had indeed procured him a helmet and skates. Unfortunately, the helmet was mustard yellow and the skates were of an era that predated the boy and maybe even the game of hockey itself, he thought. Tube skates. You know the ones; timeworn leather with tubes of metal poking out from the soles. It was better than nothing, and it brought the boy closer than he had ever been to the game. But it was impossible to hide from the pangs of embarrassment. He knew how different he'd look. That, coupled with the fact that he was about to start hockey at thirteen alongside well tenured players by that point, he almost turned away and tried to convince himself that he didn't really want to play. But that would have been a lie.

Picture this: it's the first day of hockey camp. Players stand eager and ready to start drills and skills. Among them, a lanky thirteen-year-old boy, decked out in a yellow helmet with screws missing and paint chipping, wearing holey, mismatched hockey socks that had belonged to someone during The Great Depression, and a fancy pair of faded brown leather tube skates. We're not even going to talk about the gloves.

But none of that mattered. The boy was on the ice. The stick in his hands was no longer a branch. It was a real, true to size hockey stick. He was a hockey player. At least, that's how he felt.

The practice unfolded about as well as you'd imagine. He couldn't stop. He barely turned on his own, and using edges was a laughable affair for the players and parents alike. Except for one parent. She wasn't laughing. She was thinking. Unbeknown to the boy, this experienced hockey mom left the arena and hurried home. When she returned the practice was over and the boys were changing. As the boy was leaving, carrying an old military canvas style ruck turned hockey bag, she stopped him.

"Excuse me... Matthew. That's your name, right?"

"Yes, ma'am."

"Here—try these. They should fit."

The woman handed the boy a pair of modern era skates. Gently used.

"Tyler outgrew them. But I think they'll fit you."

He was embarrassed... grateful... sheepish.

"Thank you. Um... I don't have any money..."

The woman smiled. "Don't you worry about that. They're yours now."

I wish I could give you a movie ending for all this. But as we discussed earlier; reality is often vastly different from what we craft in our own minds. The boy... Matthew... was me. The mother who gave me skates, I wish I could recall her name. But years have erased it. Her kindness, however, that I remember in perfect detail. I didn't become much of a hockey player, but I did get to play the game for a couple of years. Even a year or two with my very best friend in life. I wasn't any good, but he'd pass me the puck anyways. Thanks, Drew.

We didn't get the win against the united boys in blue. But that's all right. Because what we did get to do, was cheer on a bunch of kids that grew into adults that now play the game they've always loved. We got to watch poetry on ice. And written in the cursive of each line in the ice, is a reminder that dreams really can come true. Big and small.

Here's to the next game — and to those still chasing pucks . . . and dreams.

Matthew Heneghan is a Canadian author, decorated veteran, and host of the Unwritten Chapters *podcast. His work explores trauma, resilience, and hope, often drawing from his experiences as a military and civilian medic. His memoir,* Woven in War, *is available globally through major booksellers.*

The Cougars of TikTok

ROBYN DINER

I'm scrolling through TikTok when I come across this young white guy who's lip-synching to the song that I lost my virginity to over thirty-five years ago. As he mouths the words to Boston's "More Than a Feeling," it's like he just stepped out of a shiny, new suburban shopping mall, one that still smells of Juicy Fruit gum and hope. With feathered blonde hair to his shoulders, dude's all genetic lottery winner vibes seeped in nostalgia. I feel like the ghost of a *Teen Beat* centrefold from the 80s is haunting my algorithm. The guy can't be much older than 20 and I wonder if it's weird that my grown ass fifty-something self finds him adorable. His username is Whiteyy18, and since I'm a professor who often teaches courses on identity, social media and contemporary culture, I give myself permission to watch more videos—a lot more videos. Over and over again, for hours. The date is May 21, 2021. The next ten nights passed by in a haze.

Night 1:

I learn that Whiteyy18's actual name is William White, so he's not at all playing ironically with whiteness as an identity category. Though he is, in fact, 21—If anybody's wondering. And he's Canadian! A landscaper from Niagara, he also plays competitive hockey because of course he does. Whitey doesn't do the dances that made TikTok famous. Rather, he mostly just lip syncs to classics from the time when radio was how GenX got music.

I also discover that there's a thing called #cougartok: a hashtag that unites single women over forty-ish who prefer to engage with the TikTok content of younger men, and younger men who make content with cougars in mind. Who knew? #cougartok is mostly straight, white, western, and framed as playful. Songs like "Stacey's Mom" and anything to do with Nicole Kidman make everybody a little giddy.

When it comes to Whitey, many of his 200,000 followers are Canadian woman over 50. They fill his comments section with emoji: fire, kisses and Canadian flags explode across his page. The cougars appear divided as to what to do with him. Some want to feed him, some want to fuck him. A few even offer to e-transfer him money for no reason. And everybody begs to see pictures of his dad.

There's an academic essay waiting to be written here about aging women and heterosexual desire—one that explores memory, music and the figure of the young male body. Framed in a Canadian context, I think I might even be able to get some research money. I give myself permission to watch a bunch more Whitey content, as if any one of Canada's funding agencies is going to give me money to write that essay.

Night 2:

Whitey starts making videos to Barry Manilow's "Mandy"— and it's the sweetest kind of cringe. "Mandy," Whitey pretends to croon to Manilow's tune about love gone astray. But he's looking right into my screen—at me. He winks. He rolls his eyes upward like loving me is killing him in the best way. I feel like the prettiest girl at the all-ages disco.

Night 3:

"Mandy" is a huge hit! Whitey now has 300,000 new followers bringing him to about 500,000 overall. Even though I'm born and bred in Québec, I feel a surprising surge of national pride for him and his exploding follower count. *"Allez Whitey,"* I think to myself as he comes out with a new video sporting a red and white hockey jersey, "Go go go."

A bunch of toxic TikTok bros emerge from the manosphere to weigh in. With usernames such as @lonely_male_epidemic00, @daddy69, and @XXX123456, they clutch their man pearls and scream about reverse-sexism while calling the cougars old, ugly, saggy, wrinkly and run through—as they continue to ignore the mirrors in their mothers' basements.

A chorus of cougars reply by calmly explaining that

sexism is rooted in power structures that don't simply reverse. Others add that due to agism, the cougars are reacting to the process of becoming invisible. Demonized for simply existing as aging women in public, they are creating their own exciting online community spaces like—but not necessarily limited to—#cougartok. And there is no shame in that.

Coming out of the mouths of middle-aged women with no more microfucks left to give, the overall spirit of the response goes something like: Who asked you? You are the very reason we are all divorced, not-on-Tinder and spending our evenings watching Whitey videos. There's no way in hell we'll give up on the little pleasures that menopause hasn't already wrung out of our always exhausted night-sweaty bodies because of a bunch of motherfuckers like you, *Brad69*. Go away!

On many levels, the cougars are not wrong. Whitey in his straight, white maleness is hardly an oppressed Canadian, and he seems to be enjoying his newfound fame. But I can't help feeling like this is all far from ideal. Why are young men like Whitey making TikToks for women three decades older to ogle? Undeniably, there's a whole lot of potentially harmful objectification and self-commodification going on here in cougarland. Is Whitey OKAY? Should I worry? Is it patronizing to admit that my inner Jewish mom would be relieved to see Whitey in dental school, flourishing somewhere outside of the middle-age female gaze?

Yet, what about the part of me that is lurking about #cougartok obsessively? Am I okay? Are the cougars? Is there a way for me to explore all this without sounding like I'm scolding myself or the cougars for failing to age "gracefully," off-screen and out of the comments section silent and partnered in age-appropriate ways.

Also why am I—and so many others—this hyped at hearing Mandy back in play? Sure, the song sounds like a taste of sugar, but if you listen closely to the lyrics, they're a bleak reminder of quintessential 70s sexism. Manilow paints a picture of Mandy as the perfect girl because she offers him everything—and asks for nothing in return. Yet, as he sings, he still somehow tires of her selflessness and sends her packing. When he inevitably changes his mind and wants her back, she's no longer to be found. Although Barry does seem genuinely sad and sorry, there is never any doubt as to why he's truly upset. Indeed, what can be more tragic than losing a girl who only wants to give?

I feel like I may have some good questions going on here, like I should maybe even be jotting down some notes —but then l get distracted when I learn that Whitey's follower count has climbed to about 600,000 overnight. The Americans, the Australians, the Brits and the odd Kiwi can now be found in the comments.

Night 4:

#lesbiantok has joined the party! Making videos that consist of themselves dreamily watching Whitey lip synching, many caption their content with statements such as, "Yeah well I know I'm a lesbian, but I mean, damn!" I count the ways I could subject my imaginary essay to a queer twist and watch several more videos, just to be sure.

Night 5:

Whitey starts a TikTok Live where he simply reads comments and answers questions from fans as they appear across his screen. Sitting on a grey Ikea couch in a teal t-shirt that makes his blue eyes appear surreal, he can't stop blushing. The cougars have questions like: Do you plan to play pro hockey? Do you have a girlfriend? Do you want a girlfriend? What is your coffee order at Tim's? But mostly, especially in the case of the Canadian cougars, they thank him for the bits of joy he's bringing into their lives. He replies by saying, "No...thank you, thank you, thank you. Ladies, I'm overwhelmed." Then he blushes some more.

Overall, Whitey appears so humble, so darling, so polite—so quintessentially mythically Canadian in a way that many Canadians actually are not, that I wonder if the cougars could get the Liberal government to hire Whitey to do an ad campaign promoting Canada? Ideally, the job would even come with full benefits and a pension. Maybe the Liberals could also find Whitey a black and an Indigenous friend for the sake of diversity—but they could pay the friends twice as much as Whitey, for the sake of reparations that can never be repaid?

Night 6:

A cougar rallying cry goes out: *Ladies, many of us have made it through childbirth, shit marriages, worse jobs and a culture that mostly valued us for our fertility and fuckability but also hated us for our fertility and fuckability and now just hates us because they no longer want to fuck us. Yet here we are! Still capable of feeling pleasure, of expressing joy! Together, we can do anything! Let's get Whitey to a million followers!*

Night 7:

Whitey does another TikTok Live. This time he tells his female fans, "I know you love watching my videos, but please don't forget to go to work." Around 750,000 people are now following Whitey while working or not-working.

Night 8:

Everybody is ecstatic. Not only is Whitey close to 950, 000 followers, he's managed to sign a modelling contract with Hugo Boss! And Mr. Barry Manilow himself has made an Instagram re-posting a clip of one of Whitey's TikToks, captioned with a written shoutout out to @whiteyy18. Somehow, a group of senior citizens in their late 60s and early 70s in Florida has also found their way into this loop, and they're throwing a white party in Whitey's honour. Dressed in their best white linen, the mixed-gender crowd slow dances to tunes from the 50s on the beach in Boca Raton, while somebody's grandchild turns bits of their soirée into TikToks.

Night 9:

I go out to dinner with Eliana and Carlos. They're a couple

that have been living mindfully since way before Montreal bars started serving eighteen dollar mocktails to vegans who meditate. I try my best to draw them down the #cougartok-meets-whitey rabbit hole hoping they might have some insights into this new obsession of mine. Instead, they look at me like I just told them that, after years of sobriety, I've started putting Bailey's in my coffee—but only in the morning. I stop talking.

Later that night, Whitey gets to 1 million followers! The cougars are beyond pleased with themselves, with Whitey, with Canada, with Hugo Boss, with Barry Manilow—and with TikTok. Caught up in the moment, I feel their elation. Truly, without irony.

Night 10:

I tell myself it's time to pursue something new. I vow to delete TikTok, to go to the gym, to go on a hike, to touch grass, to let go. Instead, I find myself wandering aimlessly around my empty apartment mouthing the fucking lyrics to "Mandy."

Dr. Robyn Diner *teaches Literature at Vanier College in Montréal, Canada. She recently published "Cuddle Me Outside" in* Heavens to Murgatroyd, *which features the same MC that appears in "The Cougars of TikTok." Both of these stories intersect with a short story collection that she's working on titled* BadassTeacherLady: Tales From the Classroom and Beyond.

Old Earl Till

CINDY WEBB MORRIS

There once lived a crusty bachelor named Old Earl Till. Round the bend from no one else, deep in the backwoods of New Brunswick, squatted his two-room tar-paper shack. An outhouse in the forest nearby; wood piled by the door, and a creek behind his home satisfied his solitary life.

In the room at the back of his musty shack, covered in a stained quilt Earl had bought at the New-To-You store in town, an ancient bed sagged to the floor. He scrounged the dump at Bald Peak and found a perfectly preserved porcelain pitcher decorated with faded violets. That treasure topped a washstand Earl built himself from a spruce tree he'd felled. The front room consisted of a small icebox from the 1920's, a dented card table, and two creaky chairs. He drew a bucket of water every day from the creek for drinking, bathing, and washing the few chipped dishes he possessed. Earl figured himself lucky that the creek flowed freely all year. A tiny wood stove hunkered across from the icebox.

No one up and down the Tobique knew where the old fella came from originally. Rumour had it he just showed up in the area driving a rattly rusted Ford pickup sometime after World War Two claiming to be a veteran. The dented brown footlocker with Canadian Army and Pte Earl Till on the back of the truck confirmed his service. His scraggly grey beard and bald noggin sealed his senior citizenship.

"He does git checks from the government," the postman, Murray Babbidge, related to everyone at the Legion after Earl arrived. "The old man always has a two-four chillin' in the creek and serves me a quart bottle of Moosehead every time I stop in. He'll chat your ear off if ya git to know him." Since Old Earl didn't make any effort to be involved in the community, never attended a shiveree or a Legion meat draw, community members just shook their heads in disbelief and left Earl to himself.

"He doesn't even shop here," slurred one old-timer.

"Yeah," slobbered another. "He sneaks over to Saint-Quentin."

Earl didn't necessarily long for human company. However, he was delighted when a scrawny white kitten showed up on his doorstep one sunny spring day. After turning the animal over and looking at its nether regions, Earl declared. "I'll call you Tom. Tom Cat." And that was the beginning of their adventures together.

After training the cat to do his business outside, Old Earl taught him what he considered a most useful skill. When he showed the postman on his next visit, Murray couldn't wait to share the news at the next meat draw.

"By Jaysus, I swear to God. Not a word of a lie. Earl just whistled and that cat trotted over to the icebox and opened the door. He grabbed a bottle of beer in his paws and put it on the table. Then, Holy Mother of God, Tom Cat stood on his hind legs, put the cap in his mouth, gnawed his way around it, snapped it off and it fell to the floor. Damn, it was like he was a bottle opener."

"Oh, go on with ya'," yelled one young fella. "Can't be done." And the crowd exploded in laughter.

"No, ya' friggin' losers. It's true. And, that's not all." Murray adjusted his suspenders and glared at the folks gathered round him. "That damn cat started tattooing on Earl's bongo drum like he was Ringo Starr."

Every week, Murray would report on the many new things Tom Cat had learned: folds the paper up after Earl is finished and puts it in the wood box; lifts the kettle off the stove and makes tea; and on and on it went.

Murray was a bachelor as well and thoroughly enjoyed the time he spent with Old Earl. They both were into conspiracy theories about the aliens living among them, and often debated over whether politicians or royalty were shapeshifting lizards. Murray believed they were worms encased in human form, while Earl was firmly on the side of the lizards.

"God damn it, Earl. Let's talk about something serious for a change," Murray said one early spring morning. The pair were sitting on tree stumps a few feet away from the rising creek, enjoying the earthy scent of petrichor that followed the night's rain. Tom Cat splayed out belly up on the ground beside them. "TC wants some scratchin', Earl."

"I see that," said Old Earl as he plopped his boot in the cat's belly and rubbed it back and forth. He sighed and looked over at Murray. "So, what do you want to talk about?"

"Well, how about life and death?"

"Life and death?"

"Yeah, I'd like to know more about ya. Where ya from? Favourite singer? How do ya want to die?

Old Earl scowled at his friend. "How do I want to die? Jeepers buddy. You're a friggin' strange one for sure."

Murray chuckled. "My Grammy used to say it was because I was born in a mud puddle in the dooryard during a heavy storm."

Earl closed his eyes and murmured. "Okay, listen up. I had a fair t' middlin' life. Isn't a long story." He opened his eyes and stared into the rushing water. "I was born in

Quispamsis before it was even a village. My mother was Scottish and my father was a member of the Maliseet First Nations."

"Wait, hold on there. You're a half-breed?"

"Métis, buddy."

"Yeah, sorry," Murray said quietly, "you're so white."

"Took after my mother in looks, idiot. Followed my father into the army. He died in The Great War."

"The Great War?"

Old Earl threw up his hands. "Do you want me to tell my story or not?"

"Yeah, please."

"Okay, the Great War was WWI if you remember from history class. When my father died, my mother moved us to Woodstock and that's where I joined the army. Carleton and York regiment. I fought in WWII and came home. Many didn't."

"So, what'd ya do in the war?"

"Killed people. Don't want to talk about it." Earl gazed at the heavens. "Don't ask me again."

Murray nodded.

"When I left the army, I just wanted to be alone. And I was until you became the postman and started dropping in. And then Tom, of course." Earl pointed to the cat who was now snoring away at his feet. "You and Tom Cat came along when I was feeling lonely. I can tolerate you both. But no others, you understand."

"Message received," said Murray. "Well, better finish my route."

"Sure thing," said Earl. "Take a couple for the road." He handed two quarts to his friend and waved goodbye.

Murray turned back. "Thanks for the booze. Just tell me. How'd ya want to die?"

Earl laughed. "In my sleep, my friend, in my sleep. How about you?"

"Same here, buddy," Murray said as he drove off.

Well, it happened one July, Murray took off for his annual fishing holiday on the Miramachi. He was gone for a month and on his return to duty, he saw that his replacement had being stuffing Earl's mail into the battered metal mailbox at the edge of the road. Murray took the mail out of the box and hummed *King of the Road* while he parked his truck in the dooryard. When he got close to the door of the shack, he stopped mid-verse. The smell seeping out from the shack made him gag.

Christ, smells like bear bait, he thought. Murray remembered the putrid odor from the days he accompanied his father collecting offal from farmers for use in the hunting season. He pulled his sweater up over his nose and gingerly opened the door.

"Hello," he said in a muffled voice. "You there, Earl?" No answer. He could see from the doorsill the bachelor was lying on his bed in the next room. Murray shuffled over to discover a bloated body crawling in blow flies and some kind of black beetle. He recognized Earl's clothing but nothing else. Teeth and hair were falling away from the corpse. There was no nose.

Murray turned around to run out the door when he spied Tom Cat resting in the corner. Is he dead too? *I better check,* he thought. He leaned down and was struck with the noxious fumes of alcohol. That's when Murray spotted the dozen empty bottles of beer by the cat's side. What a mess. He touched the cat to find it dead cold. When something fell out of its mouth, he jumped back in horror. It was a nose. He could see from the hairy nostrils that it was Earl's nose. *I think Earl got his wish but Tom died from alcohol poisoning, for sure,* he thought.

Murray regaled the boozers that night. "Tom Cat must have partied hardy after Earl died."

"Poor thing," said one of the ladies. "He was probably grieving for Earl."

The story of Old Earl Till and Tom Cat might have ended right there, but it became a legend and like many legends, it got stranger over time. If you want to know the truth, sit on a stump anywhere on the banks of the Tobique River, and the pair of them will join you. They'll tell you their tale for a tip of your hat and a couple quarts of Moosehead.

Cindy Webb Morris, *born and raised in New Brunswick, has lived in Toronto, Ottawa, Vancouver, Yellowknife, and now makes her home in Calgary. Her published efforts include a personal essay, poems, newspaper articles, and short stories. She is currently working on the final draft of her first novel.*

Main Street Wanderings

JOY L. MAGNUSSON

S mall town Alberta is a magical place. Some people may laugh when they glance down Main Street in some little town where heavy traffic consists of five cars, two of which are parked. But if they were to stop for just a minute and really listen, they might find out there's a lot more going on than they thought.

I remember that day I stood at the top of Main Street with Granny Dot and Great-Aunt Florrie. It was so perfectly quiet and peaceful there in the warm sun. The perfect place for a visit with my family.

I'd taken some time that summer to get out of the city and go to Granny's acreage to help her with her garden and yard work. On this particular day, we had taken a break to join Aunt Florrie on her afternoon walk. And, as I stood there with these two dear ladies in this tiny little town they'd grown up in, I got curious.

"Granny Dot, has anything interesting ever happened to anyone in our family?"

"Interesting?" Granny asked, "What do you mean?"

"Well," I said, "Has anyone ever had any interesting adventures or done anything extraordinary?"

Granny began walking slowly as she thought, and Aunt Florrie and I followed.

"Well, I don't really–"

"Look, Dottie!" Aunt Florrie said suddenly, "Can you believe it's still here?"

She was standing right next to the new bank they'd built just that spring. The building that used to be on that lot had sported a concrete stoop in front for longer than I could remember. The shiny new bank had been designed with the main entrance on the corner. So, the crumbling stoop had been removed.

Now, Aunt Florrie stared at the grey, discoloured square patch where the stoop had been. Etched into its aging surface were several names. Some were disappearing with the damaged edges of the age-old slab, but one in particular grabbed my eye.

"Hey!" I said, pointing, "That's Great-Grandfather's name, isn't it?"

"It sure is," Granny said proudly, "Florrie and I stood right here and watched him scratch it in the wet cement the year he brought it up here."

"Brought what up here?" I asked.

"Well, the town, of course. He brought it up here from the

valley. Didn't you know?"

I stared at Granny Dot, confused.

"He brought the whole town—"

"To be fair," Aunt Florrie said quickly, "It wasn't the whole town. Remember, the old ice house was washed away that last summer."

"Wait," I stammered, "What do you mean—"

"True," Granny nodded, "But still, if it weren't for him ..."

"Granny," I finally said a little more loudly, "What are you talking about? What do you mean, Great-Grandfather brought the town up here?"

Granny and Aunt Florrie exchanged surprised looks.

"No one's ever told you about that?" Aunt Florrie asked me.

"No." I shrugged. "I guess not."

"Well," Granny stretched her arms wide, "this was not the town's first location." She pointed off toward the edge of town, where the row of buildings gave way to an open field that sloped down into a grove of trees, "It used to be down there."

I squinted at the distant evergreens.

"Where?"

"Have you ever walked from your cousin Katie's house along the trail that leads down to the lake?"

"Sure," I said, "Millions of times. Katie's house is just beyond those trees. We used to go down to the lake all the time when we were kids."

"Well," Granny said, "that trail used to be Main Street."

"What?" I looked back toward that end of town, "That trail is just a foot path stomped through the woods down to the water. How could it have possibly been Main Street?"

Granny and Aunt Florrie had started walking down the street again.

"Well, it's grown over a bit, since then," Granny said, "But, at one time, it was a fine, wide gravel road with the post office, grocery, and bakery running up one side–"

"–and the stable, and doctor's office on the other," Aunt Florrie added.

"And the hotel," Granny said. "Don't forget the old Holskie Hotel."

"How could I?" Aunt Florrie chuckled. "The way Father handled that whole affair had the town talking for years!"

"Wait a minute," I finally interjected. "Please, start at the beginning. I mean, why would you want to move a whole town?"

"Frogs," Aunt Florrie said matter-of-factly, as if that single word clearly explained everything.

"That's right," Granny nodded, "That and Tanner Cook's barn door."

This time, I just waited quietly. I figured maybe they'd tell the story quicker if I left them to it.

They didn't disappoint.

"The lake has shrunk a bit since then," Aunt Florrie began, "but back in those days, town was right near the lake shore."

"I suppose when Harold Smeckers chose that spot for a new post office a few years earlier, it must have seemed like the ideal spot," Granny said. "It was only a short distance to the railroad tracks, so it would be easy for the postmaster to pick up the mail at the train station, and the creek would provide plenty of fresh water."

"It wasn't long, though, before the postmaster added a general store to the post office. Then a blacksmith's shop was opened and a church established. The next thing you know, we had a whole new town. And as more people set up homes and businesses, it became alarmingly clear that Mr. Smeckers hadn't picked such a perfect spot, after all."

"That close to the lake, the land was very boggy and marshy," Granny explained. "Not a suitable place for a town at all, really. Every spring, everyone's cellars would fill with water, and frogs and other swamp life would just infest Main Street. We'd find frogs in our houses and in the stores. Oh, it was just a mess."

"Yes," Aunt Florrie added, "But we'd more or less learned to live with that. For a couple of years, at least."

Granny nodded, "For a couple of years. Right until Mr. Terrance moved onto the Rise."

We were at the end of the street now, overlooking the sprawling field east of town. In the distance, I could just see the faint path that vanished into the thick grove of trees, below, on its way to the lake.

Granny pointed to a sharp slope of the far side of the former Main Street. The top of the sharp incline was bordered by a thin row of trees.

"Mr. Terrance lived up there," she said, "right above the town. His wife and children seemed like nice enough folks. But Mr. Terrance was a nasty, stubborn old man. Determined to have everything his own way, no matter what."

"Mm-hmm," Aunt Florrie agreed, "That's why he destroyed all those trees in the first place. He wanted to have the best view in the county. And from up there on the Rise overlooking the lake, he might have had it, too. Come."

With that last word, Aunt Florrie motioned us across the road so we could walk back down Main Street on the other side.

"Well, the following spring," Aunt Florrie continued, "when all the snow melted and the rain started falling, the trees weren't there to hold back any of the runoff, and all the water poured down the embankment and right into Main Street. It was like a new river had popped up and set its course right through the middle of town. It was way worse than it had ever been before."

"It happened to some degree every time another thunderstorm rolled through here, that year." Granny added, "We'd just clean up one mess and another storm would blow through. Everyone was just furious with Mr. Terrance. Some people wouldn't even talk to him for the longest time."

"Well," Aunt Florrie continued, "that summer turned into autumn, and by winter we'd about forgotten about the whole thing. Then, one morning the following April—Was it April, Dottie?"

"I think so, dear."

"Well, that morning, Mayor McCracken stepped off his front porch and right up to his shins in ice-cold water."

"Mm–hmm," Granny Dot said, "We'd had an unexpected warm spell and nearly overnight most of the snow on the Rise had melted and the whole town was flooded out, again."

"Yes," Aunt Florrie added, "Father told us that the mayor said the whole town looked like a brand-new lake with a few houses sticking out of it."

"Good grief," I muttered, trying to picture that.

"That's when the mayor heard the happy shrieks of children." Granny shook her head. "He turned around just in time to see three or four of the Crocker children sailing down Main Street on a big raft which, until just that morning, had been the door to Mr. Crocker's barn. Mr. Crocker might have been mad about that, too, if he wasn't too busy chasing his wife's laundry basket downstream to notice. Well, Mayor McCracken decided right that second that something needed to be done. He was determined that we wouldn't go through another season of this."

"Right," Granny agreed, "Well, our house was far enough from town that it was reasonably dry."

"We also had some extra space since Father had added those extra rooms the year before."

"Right. So, Father offered our living room as a town meeting space until the town hall could be bailed out. Mother sent Florrie and me up to bed early to get us out of the way. So, naturally, we listened from the hallway."

"Naturally," agreed Aunt Florrie. "Everyone was there. Even Mr. Terrance. A lot of people didn't want him there, but somehow, the Reverend John talked them into it. Brotherly love and all that."

"Brotherly love, indeed! They argued all night long." Granny cringed and waved her hands as though waving off the long-ago shouting voices. "Mr. Richmond wanted to buy a big pump to force all the water into the lake. But the mayor said it would be too costly. And some people thought it would be too noisy, too. Someone else suggested building a wall on the Rise where the trees used to be, but Mr. Terrance refused.

Didn't want anything to block his precious view, I suppose."

"Yes," said Aunt Florrie. "Mr. Crocker even suggested that Mr. Terrance ought to be responsible for cleaning up the mess since he was the one who had caused it. Well, I'll tell you, tempers really started flying then! There were shouting and threats. Father had to come between Mr. Crocker and Mr. Terrance to keep them from coming to blows!"

Aunt Florrie stopped there. We were about halfway up the other side of the street, and both of them were a little breathless.

"Sit here for a minute," I said, leading them to a little wooden bench right outside Tucker's Everything Shop. The building cast a nice shadow over them, giving them a break from the warm summer sun.

"Well, what happened next?" I asked, sitting next to them.

"What?" Granny asked. They both looked at me quizzically.

"The meeting," I reminded them, "about the flooding town."

"We knew what you were asking," Aunt Florrie said gently. "We were just wondering if you might get us a little water before we continue."

"Of course!" I jumped to my feet, a little embarrassed that I hadn't thought of that myself. "I'll be right back."

I stepped into the Everything Shop and quickly glanced around at the large, cluttered selection of merchandise until I spotted the fridge in the corner by the checkout counter. I opened it and grabbed three bottles of water and a bag of fresh raspberries. Then I turned to the kindly-faced old man who was operating the cash register.

"Hi there," he smiled, taking my purchases, "Are they your family?" He motioned to the open window where the tops of Granny and Aunt Florrie's sun hats were just visible over the ledge.

"Yes," I told him. "Dot is my granny."

"Oh," he said cheerfully. "How nice. Dear old ladies, those two. I've known them since we were all kids."

He paused a minute like he was trying to decide whether to continue.

"I confess I overheard part of your conversation," he said in a hushed voice, "but you should know, your granny and aunt may be exaggerating, just a bit."

I glanced at the window, suddenly grateful for their weakened hearing.

"About what?" I asked.

"Well, for one thing, Granddad and Mr. Crocker did not almost come to blows. They'd never lay a hand on each other."

"Oh! So, Mr. Terrance was your grandfather?"

"That he was," said the old man, "and let me tell you, he didn't take those trees down because he wanted a view." He shook his head firmly.

"Then why–"

He tipped his head toward the window. "For them."

"For Granny Dot and Aunt Florrie?"

"Well, them and their eight brothers and sisters. You see, when their folks came to this area, they had only themselves and their two oldest to take care of, so their father only built his family a small cabin. But it wasn't long before Dottie and Florrie, and the others came along. Their father knew he needed more room, but with so many kids to feed, he just didn't have the cash for the lumber he'd need. My granddad had plenty of timber on his land, so he offered to trade some trees in exchange for a few weeks' worth of work during harvesting time. Granddad was like that. Always looking out for his neighbour."

"Granny Dot and Aunt Florrie never told me that!"

"Near as I know, they were never told. You see, when my granddad decided he could spare those trees along the edge of the Rise, he had no idea their removal would cause so much trouble. He was quite embarrassed about the whole affair, of course. But what really bothered him was the idea of hurting Dottie and Florrie's family. He was afraid that if people knew that those trees had been removed for their benefit, they'd be run out of town. So, Granddad and their father agreed to keep silent."

"But why wouldn't he let them build up a wall to stop the flooding?"

"Didn't feel it would be right to let the town spend any money on his land after the damage he'd caused. But he couldn't afford to build a wall himself, either. That's when he and Dottie and Florrie's Father cooked up their idea."

"What idea?" I asked eagerly.

"Where are you, dear?" Granny Dot's voice floated through the window. I'd gotten so wrapped up in the old man's story, I'd forgotten about bringing out the water.

"Gotta go," I told the old man quickly. "Thanks."

I grabbed my things off the counter and hurried back out to the sidewalk.

"Sorry," I told them as I unscrewed the lids and handed them each a bottle of cold water. We didn't talk much as we all drank and picked raspberries from the bag. But as soon as we were ready to start walking, again, I asked, "So what was

Great-Grandfather's idea?"

They stared at me.

"At the meeting. What idea did Great-Grandfather suggest for dealing with the flooding?"

"Well, not much." Granny said. "People really didn't listen to our father, you know. He was nearly blind and, in those days, people thought a blind person wasn't really much use. So, father was largely ignored at town gatherings like that."

"He tried to suggest that the town could be moved to a higher, dryer spot without much trouble," Aunt Florrie explained, "But they didn't want to listen." She shook her head kind of sadly, "I still remember the way the mayor told him to just hush and let the men talk."

Even though I never knew him, my cheeks still burned at the thought of anyone talking to my great-grandfather that way.

"So, they left that meeting without a plan in place," Granny went on, "It just seemed like it was hopeless. We'd just have to live with the spring floods until the trees grew back."

Just then, we reached the corner by the grocery store. Granny reached over and gently touched the purple petals of a pansy growing in one of the street planters.

"Oh, aren't they lovely this year?" she said to Aunt Florrie.

"Yes, indeed. I understand from Leslie that the committee ordered them from that new greenhouse in Cold Lake."

"Oh, really? I was told– So, what happened?" I finally prompted, trying to remain patient. "How did the town get up here?"

"Well, it was the town picnic," Aunt Florrie said as we passed the flowers, "Oh, Mother made her delicious apple-cinnamon pie that year. Do you remember, Dottie?"

"No one made pies quite like our mother." Granny told me, "I can still smell them baking in the kitchen as fresh as if she'd just baked one this minute."

She and Aunt Florrie were practically licking their lips.

"We used to have our picnics up here, in the spring, back when it was still a meadowland," Granny stopped and looked around Main Street as if still seeing the field of swaying grass dotted by blankets and picnic baskets with all their long-ago neighbours talking and laughing with each other, "Those were wonderful days."

"Yes," Aunt Florrie smiles dreamily.

"It was right about three in the afternoon when one of the Terrance kids came running up from the town site, yelling, 'He's coming! He's coming!' Well, we all dropped what we were doing and rushed to that end of the meadow to see what was happening. And wouldn't you know it? Here comes our father, right up the trail."

"And he looked pleased as punch sitting on top of that hotel like the king of the castle."

"What?" I asked, nearly dropping my own water, "On top of a hotel?"

"He'd rigged it up to an axel device on wheels," said Aunt Florrie. "Then he had the whole thing pulled right up the slope by a team of tractors and horses all being driven by men from around the town. He couldn't drive due to his vision, of course. So, he was sitting on top of the porch roof holding the reins and grinning, proud as could be. Oh, you should have seen it, dear. The whole town was cheering and jumping up and down. Even the mayor was clapping his hands like a little boy! Everyone was so excited! Everyone except old Mr. Terrance, of course. He was the only one leaning against a tree, quietly smoking his pipe and being his old, cranky self."

"Yes," Granny added. "Seems after the meeting, Father met up with some of the other men in town and worked the whole thing out. He reminded them that the town wouldn't last very long in those conditions. They didn't want to have to resort to travelling all the way to the next town for groceries and supplies. They also didn't want to wait for the town's politicians to quit bickering and actually do something about the problem. So, they eagerly agreed to Father's plan."

"And since the mayor and the councilmen wouldn't listen to what Father had to say," Aunt Florrie said, "he decided to just go ahead and show 'em."

"What if the town hadn't liked the idea?" I asked.

"Never crossed Father's mind." Granny told me, "He was a very determined man. Never met a barrier he couldn't overcome."

"True." Aunt Florrie nodded. "And he was right. The mayor loved the idea. So, they bought the land, got the permits, and hired Father to move the whole town up the hill to this very spot."

We were now back at the top of Main Street where we'd started.

"And at the end of that summer," Aunt Florrie said, "when they had finished bringing the town up here, Father and the whole crew of movers were allowed to sign their names in the freshly poured sidewalk right in front of the first building they'd brought up here."

"Wow." I stared down the street, trying to imagine the scene: Great-Grandfather riding that hotel up the hill like a king, everyone celebrating wildly, and the day finally won by the most useless man in town.

Granny stopped, looking suddenly puzzled, like she'd lost something. Then she turned to me. "I'm sorry, dear. Were you asking me something before? Just when we started our walk?"

I had to laugh.

"Yes, Granny. I was just asking whether anyone in our family ever had any interesting adventures or accomplished anything special."

Granny thought for a minute. "No," she finally said slowly, "I can't think of anything. They've all just been ordinary, hard-working people. Nothing special. I'm sorry if that disappoints you. Can you think of anything, Florrie?"

Aunt Florrie shook her head.

I stared at my Granny and Aunt Florrie.

"Anyway," Granny said, turning toward Aunt Florrie's house, "we should head back now. It'll be time to start dinner soon."

Aunt Florrie followed her, and as they walked away, I heard Granny saying, "You know, we never did figure out where Father got the equipment for the moving rig."

"Nope. Always said it was of no consequence."

With a jolt of realization, I looked back down the street toward the Everything Store as the old man's words came floating back to me.

That's when he and Dottie, Flo, and Florrie's father had cooked up their idea.

I had to smile. Mr. Terrance wasn't being grumpy when Great-Grandfather brought that hotel up the hill. He was just graciously stepping aside.

Well, Mr. Terrance, you did it, didn't you? You made your amends.

Joy L. Magnusson is a freelance writer based in Edmonton, Alberta. She has had articles in national and international publications, and is always looking for new opportunities. She loves writing about nature and history and is currently working on her first novel. Please find her at www.joyandwriting.com.

Reconciling

SHAWN L. BIRD

Kirsten Redfeather joined our grade nine class on the fifteenth of September. The rest of us had settled into the Canterbury High routines and already formed into our friend groups, when we came into English after lunch and found a stranger sitting in Ashley Smith's spot.

"You can't sit there," said Ashley. "That's my spot."

The new girl looked right through her and didn't move a millimetre.

Mr. Petrie came through the door then, his fluorescent green World's Greatest Teacher coffee mug in hand.

"Sir! There's someone in my seat!" Ashley glared at him, with all fourteen years of fury blazing in her eyes. Ashley sat in the second seat of the middle row in every one of her classes. Everyone knew that. On the first day of class, we always left that spot for her.

"Ah!" said Mr. Petrie, smiling at the new girl. "I received a message that we'd have a new student today. Kirsten Redfeather, isn't it? Welcome. Let me get you your text books."

"Sir!" squawked Ashley.

Mr. Petrie was digging in the book cupboard behind his desk. He came up with two slightly battered books. He grabbed the textbook sign-out clipboard off its nail and deposited everything on Kirsten's desk. "Fill out the forms. The numbers are stamped on the bottom of the books." He spun around, heading to the white board and called out, "All right class, let's get going!"

"Sir!" said Ashley in an ominous growl. "Where am I supposed to sit?"

Mr. Petrie waved his hand airily. "I don't see anyone back there. That should do." The desk in question was slightly wobbly and had a loose chair bottom. No one liked to sit there. It frequently bit the sitter on the butt and the loose screws ripped long hair right out of our heads.

"But . . ." Ashley started, but Mr. Petrie cut her off.

"Let it go, Ashley. No one likes a whiner."

Ashley's eyes got huge and she puffed up indignantly. She looked like she was blinking back tears of mortification.

Desmond snickered.

Several of us gasped. It was no secret that Ashley had been crushing on Desmond Parker since grade six. We dared not look back as we heard Ashley's books thump onto the desktop.

With his attendance clipboard in his hand, Mr. Petrie glanced up and down as he checked our names off. "You know, I just realized I haven't made a formal seating plan for this class yet."

We glanced at each other. No one liked assigned seats. We liked to choose where we sat.

"I'll just record your location today," he said flipping to his seating chart of the room and scribbling our names in the little squares. "Those are your official places from now on." He was so matter-of-fact; it was like he hadn't just caused a major seismic shift in the room.

I couldn't help but glance back to Ashley. She was shooting eye-daggers alternately at Mr. Petrie and Kirsten. I exchanged looks with my BFF Dani. *Uh oh,* my glance said.

This will not go well, hers replied.

The rumours started the next day. We heard the humming in the halls: *Kirsten Redfeather is a foster kid.*

"What's wrong with that?" said Stevie. "I'm a foster kid. I don't smell or anything."

"Well," said Dani. "When you cover yourself in body spray after PE you definitely do."

"That's different," he said as he sniffed his arm pits.

"It's actually kind of gross," I said. "No one can breathe around you. But being a foster kid isn't gross. Who would possibly care about something like that?"

"Thanks," said Stevie. "You're really nice. Would you go to the Thanksgiving Dance with me?"

I hadn't seen that coming. "Ah. Sorry, no. But it's not because you're a foster kid. Hey, why don't you ask Kirsten Redfeather? That'd be a nice way to welcome her to the school."

Stevie glanced across the room to where Kirsten was talking to Mr. Petrie. "Good idea" he said. "I will."

He looked really happy afterwards, so I think she said yes.

The next rumour buzzing through the halls was *Kirsten Redfeather's father is in jail.*

"I'm pretty sure it wouldn't be her fault if he was," said Olivia.

"Jail? That's kinda cool. I wonder if he's a biker?" pondered Kevin.

"I'd really miss my dad if he was sent away," said Ryan.

"We should invite her to come to movie night, so she has something else to think about," said Kevin. "Isn't the Oldies Theatre playing *Escape from Alcatraz* this weekend?"

"Kevin!" we all said, rolling our eyes at him.

But it was, and we did. Kirsten said she'd love to come.

When Ashley heard about it, she said it was either Kirsten or her.

Ryan said we were all sorry she'd be staying home.

The next thing we heard being murmured in the halls was *Kirsten Redfeather's mother is a drunk.*

"Huh," said Lexi. "I wonder if I should invite Kirsten to come to AlAnon with me?"

"What's AlAnon?" said Desmond.

"It's a group for kids whose parents have addiction problems. It's been really helpful for me."

Desmond looked thoughtful for a moment and then leaned closer to her, "Can you text me about where to go for meetings?" I don't think he meant for me to hear.

"Sure," said Lexi, with a meaningful look at me.

I know when to keep a secret, so I drew the metaphorical zipper across my lips.

The next week *Kirsten Redfeather is a bannock eater* was scrawled across the white board when we arrived in class.

"Mmm. Bannock," said Desmond. Kirsten was just coming into the room, and he called out, "Hey Kirsten! Can you make bannock?"

"No, not really," she said. "I'm not much of a cook."

"I can," said Liz Chartrand. "My nohkom taught me."

"Yum," said Desmond. "I love it with butter and raspberry jam."

"We should have a bannock party," said Kevin. "Mr. Petrie, can Liz teach us all how to make bannock for Orange Shirt day?"

"Excellent idea," said Mr. Petrie. "Liz, tell me what you need and I'll see if Mrs. White will trade me use of her Home Ec room that day."

"Yay!" we all shouted, high fiving each other. Bannock was awesome.

"Can we learn beadwork, too?" said Olivia. "I have always wanted to learn how to do that. Do you know how, Kirsten?"

Kirsten shook her head, "No, but the First Nations support teacher at my last school gave workshops during lunch hours for everyone. Could yours show you?"

Olivia grinned, "Awesome idea!"

Mr. Petrie said, "You know, Olivia, Ms. Riel probably has

supplies. We should ask if she'll offer lunch hour sessions."

"This is amazing. Ashley! What do you want to bead?"

Ashley buried her nose in her silent reading book and ignored us.

On September thirtieth, we had English just before lunch. We all met in the Home Ec room to make bannock. We set the tables and stayed during lunch hour to eat them. Mr. Petrie brought Saskatoon jam his mom had made. Ryan brought homemade butter from his family's dairy cows. It was the best bannock ever.

After lunch we had an assembly. After the land acknowledgement, Dr. Scott, our principal, reminded us about Phyllis Webstad and the origins of Orange Shirt Day. Then he introduced the special guest speaker. It was Terrance Redfeather. He was a lawyer and he was there to share with us about Truth and Reconciliation. The whole school listened attentively as he spoke about residential schools and the cultural damage they did by removing children from their communities.

"Hey," I whispered to Kirsten, "Is that your dad?"

"Yeah," she whispered back. "I'm so embarrassed." She didn't look embarrassed, though. I thought she looked really proud of him.

After Mr. Redfeather spoke, Ms. Riel called up a group of girls in ribbon skirts to sing "The Song of the Bois-Brûlés" in French. Liz Chartrand was up there with them.

When they finished, Dani said, "That sounded sad."

"And violent," whispered Olivia, who had been in French Immersion.

"Yeah," said Kevin. "Be quiet. Here come the drummers."

"Don't be ridiculous" grumbled Ashley. "We don't need to be quiet. No one is going to have trouble hearing the drummers."

The gym filled with the pulse of the decorated hand drums the grade eleven students had made the year before. It was like the hearts of everyone in the building were synchronizing.

A group of jingle dancers came forward. "That looks fun," said Lexi. "I wish I had some kind of culture. Being English is boring."

"There are folk dances in England," said Ryan.

"Do you know any?" Lexi asked him.

"Well, no," he shrugged.

"There you go," said Lexi. "Boring."

"How come you're not with the jingle dancers?" I asked Kirsten.

She shrugged. "My brother is a serious Fancy Dance pow-wow dancer. It's intimidating because everyone thinks I'll be really good because he is."

"I get it. My brother is a scary good piano player," I said. "I can never compete. He's some kind of prodigy. If I want to play, my mom will say 'Get off the piano, sweetie. Your brother needs to practice.' I mean, he's already good! I'm the one who needs to practice."

Kirsten laughed. "Exactly. I don't compete, but I still like to dance with the aunties and cousins. It's fun when everyone joins in."

The jingle dancers had spread out and were making a giant circle around the gym as the rhythm of the drums changed.

"Everyone is supposed to join in this dance." said Kirsten, reaching past me to tap Ashley on the shoulder. "Come on, let's go."

Ashley leaned way back with a look of horror on her face. "But I don't know how."

"That's okay," said Kirsten. "You don't have to know, you just have to be willing to learn."

"But . . ." said Ashley, her eyes darting around.

"I'm going," said Desmond, reaching out a hand to pull her to her feet. "Come with me."

"Oh," said Ashley, looking from Desmond to Kirsten.

Dani smirked at me.

"I don't know how, either," I said, hooking my elbow through one of Ashley's arms as Desmond hooked his through the other, "but I think we can learn."

Shawn L. Bird is a poet and a prolific author of YA and adult novels in the beautiful Shuswap region of BC. Her novella set in Canterbury High, Murdering Mr. Edwards, *which* Outlander *author Diana Gabaldon called "Clever, funny and totally engaging," was nominated for an Arthur Ellis Crimewriting award. Visit her at ShawnBird.com*

Kindness, Canada

FINNIAN BURNETT

Magas came across the border, Perry said one day in math, and I laughed, thinking they'd said, "Maggots."

But no, they meant MAGA, red hats and blustery faces and trucks decorated with American flags and after school, we passed a group of them, drinking beer at Thomas'.

"Don't make eye contact," Sage said, but Aspen and Kai were already filming them, cameras rolling until we hit 5th Street and turned the corner.

"Welcome to Kindness," Aspen yelled back over his shoulder and then we were running, all of us, running and hollering and laughing because it was funny, at least then.

We'd forgotten about them by that evening because I had to help Perry with their math homework and Aspen and Kai were uploading content to their "Gays of our Lives" channel while Sage made dinner with Perry's moms.

The next day, though, Louis Crankston who always smiled at our group when we walked past his house locked the pawn shop early and parked his truck in front of city hall with a hand-painted sign that said, "No More Government Overreach!"

"When did the government ever reach Kindness, anyway?" Perry muttered as the twins filmed it.

Sage said to ignore it, but later, a guy in an American flag poncho started yelling about statehood in front of Betty's bakery and someone threw paint on Perry's moms' Subaru, right over the rainbow sticker.

"We should organize," Perry said, and the twins started a new channel, "Random Acts of Kindness" which should have been about kittens or bake sales, but was really just Aspen and Kai filming weird things like the old ladies at the senior centre knitting "Canada is not for sale" scarves and the dude with all the tattoos showing up to Thomas' in a rainbow hat.

"Listen," Kai said. "If we're going to live in the town with the dumbest name in the world, we're going to capitalize on it."

"We can't be the dumbest named town in the world while Wetwang, England exists," Ash said. "Besides, we're the queerest town in the world. Stop giving us more titles."

The queerest small town in Canada, someone had once called us on CBC, and it had gotten around. Perry's moms ran a bookshop, and a male couple had the coffee shop next to the fabric store, and the Gay Straight Alliance had more kids in it than the chess club, so the name stuck, and it brought a lot of queer tourism, which might have been what drew the red hats.

On Sunday, I put up my signs in the library for our monthly *pancakes and pronouns* brunch. Free to anyone in the community who wanted to eat pancakes and support the GSA. Sponsored by Mr. Bert and the curling team.

"Maybe we should cancel," Perry said when a convoy of fifteen pickup trucks did circles around the parking lot of the Oddfellows Hall and someone tore down the poster Sage had spent hours making—the one with little smiling pancakes, glittery unicorns, and drag queens with pitchers of orange juice.

I stared at the poster, run over and ruined. "Cancel," I repeated, and Perry nodded, taking my hand.

Sage crossed her arms, standing in front of the destroyed poster like it was evidence in a crime scene. "We don't cancel," she said. "We never cancel." But her voice cracked, just a little, and I wondered if she was thinking about Perry's moms and their ruined car, or the new graffiti that showed up on the wall outside of Betty's.

Aspen filmed the poster as wind caught the corner of it and half-lifted it from the ground. "If we cancel, they'll win. Kai pulled out his phone, as well, and I could almost see the new "Random Acts of Kindness" show popping up on their channel, amassing a massive following for their take on small town queers fighting back with pancakes.

"I just don't want anyone to get hurt," Perry whispered, and my stomach folded in on itself as I hugged them. "Me neither," I said.

Kai whipped his camera around to us and I mustered a smile. "Come on, everyone. The pancakes aren't going to serve themselves."

"No one's going to come," Aspen said, but he valiantly pulled out a fry pan and poured in the dough.

And no one did come, not for a while. Not that we'd ever had a huge crowd, but at least the kids from the GSA and the coffee shop guys and Mrs. Baxter who ran the flower shop. But none of them came.

Sage and I ate the first few pancakes, then took over frying duty.

"Holy hell," Kai said, as he checked his phone. "Fifteen hundred views on my last video."

And still the trucks circled our parking lot but as I peered out the window at them, I saw a mini van pull around them. Then a Volkswagen. And Mr. Karr's old Ford. And then so many people started showing up. First a few adults came in. Then half the hockey team and the entire senior class cheerleading squad. Mr. Bert smiled awkwardly from the juice table when a troupe of drag queens from the city came in, and Perry's moms brought two loaded trays full of brownies, mini pies, and cookies.

"Gawd, I love your moms' brownies," Sage said, through a mouthful of chocolate.

"Save room for more pancakes," I said.

Mr. Bert brought out a jug of maple syrup and passed it around the table and Sage and I fried pancake after pancake after pancake until Perry took over with a girl from our math class. Sage and I wandered the room, rolled up pancakes in our hands, snitching treats from the buffet table and stuffing our mouths.

And the trucks stayed on the other side of the parking lot and eventually they must have got bored and left.

"That's the end of them," Perry said, but their hands shook as they helped me dry the last of the dishes.

But it wasn't the end, not then, not by a long shot. Because that night, someone broke into the school and vandalized the GSA room. Mr. Bert found it, we heard later, and called the police, but Sage's dad works for the RCMP and one of his buddies told him someone had spray painted faggot and other words all over the walls.

If that was true, I couldn't say, because Mr. Bert cleaned up everything before we came back to school on Monday and even got the local painters in to put a fresh coat on everything so if the words had been there, I couldn't find them, not even a trace. But I believed and so did the others.

"In our home," Aspen kept repeating.

"And we didn't even get video," Kai said, though he filmed us, and even Mr. Bert, interviewing him about the police visit and the destruction.

The only remaining evidence of the attack were the broken windows, boarded up, and Kai and Aspen filmed Sage in front of them, caught her tears as she told us what she'd heard from her dad.

I zombied my way through school that day and walked home alone, taking a long block to avoid passing Thomas' where the Maga hats were still hanging out, drinking now with Mr. Crankston and a few others from town.

I texted the gang and asked them to come over. Kai and Aspen showed up and so did Sage a little bit after.

But Perry didn't respond in the group chat. Didn't even read our messages.

"We have to do something," I said. I didn't know what. I

couldn't begin to think, but energy coursed through me, making my joints ache. "This must be what a werewolf feels like before it turns," I said, laughing it off, but the twins nodded seriously like they knew.

They knew.

"We're holding a meeting at the rink tonight," Sage said, looking up from her phone. "Text everyone you can."

I texted Perry again, once in the group chat, and once solo. No answer. As the others gathered people and made plans, I texted and called and fretted.

"I'm worried," I said.

"They're probably just sick," Kai said.

"They were fine at school," Sage answered.

"We were none of us fine after what happened," I said.

We finally walked over to the bookshop on our way to the rink, hoping to at least talk to the moms. We found Perry shelving queer romances like they were in the book shelving Olympics. The moms whispered as we walked in and gave us those sympathetic looks—the kind parents give kids when they think we can't handle something.

"We're having a protest at the rink," I said, but Perry shook their head. "I'm not going."

"It's best if Perry sits this one out," Mama Jean said.

I blinked at her, stupidly like I understood the words, but I couldn't make them make sense. "Sit it out?"

"We're a lesbian couple with a trans child," Mama Jean said. "We don't need to invite more trouble."

"You don't have to invite it for it to find you," Sage said. "And maybe a lot of other people, too."

"We don't want to see you kids get hurt," Carol, Perry's

other mom, said.

The bookshop's bell chimed but I couldn't turn around, trapped by Perry's tears and by the fear on their moms' faces.

"I brought signs." Mr. Bert's voice boomed behind me. "We're going to be late if we don't head over." He held up the poster board. The first one read Welcome to Kindness with a picture of a maple leaf holding hands with a rainbow. Sage giggled next to me.

Mr. Bert shuffled his feet. "I know the artwork isn't much, but it's the heart that matters." He looked around at all of us. "I know I'm just an old straight guy. But I was born in Kindness, Canada, and I'm going to die in Kindness, Canada, and I sure as hell don't want to see it torn apart because a couple jerks don't recognize goodness when it's staring them in the face."

Perry's moms didn't speak. None of us did. And I held my breath as the world tilted and the butterflies in my stomach did a breakdance up into my throat.

"We show up," Mr. Bert finally said. And Mama Rose placed a hand on his shoulder and said, "Yes.

Carol turned to Perry. "What do you want, sweetie?"

Perry looked around at all of us, then back at their moms. "I'm so scared," they whispered. "But I want to go."

Sage and I looped our arms through Perry's, and we marched out the door. The moms locked the doors behind them and followed behind the twins. Mama Rose took Carol's hand and reached for Mr. Bert with the other. And Betty from the bakery came outside, and the woman who owns the fabric store, and that lady with the two corgis, and then the guys from the coffee shop and their neighbours, and even the guy who lives down the street who works at the plant and drives a big truck, he came out and walked with us.

And we walked back Thomas' bar and waved at the people drinking on the patio and some of them waved back. A woman stood from her table and jumped over the little fence around the patio to join our walk. Mr. Bert handed her a sign, and she held it up as she walked beside us.

"This is it," Ash yelled behind us. "This is our home."

I turned to smile at him, but the trucks caught my eye— turning off the side street on the other side of Thomas' bar and they revved their engines behind us. My body tensed as they honked and revved and some of them screeched around us. "Hey homo," one of them yelled from the window and Kai threw up a middle finger, but Mama Rose smacked it down. "We're better than that," she said.

We marched all the way down 5th and turned onto Main and then we were on Poplar Street and the trucks roared around us and the smell of exhaust nearly made me puke, but we rounded the last corner to the rink and I stopped short.

More people, more people than I even knew, stood in front of the rink. Some of them had signs.

Kindness loves.

Hate has no home here.

One sign, held barely aloft by a woman who looked to be about 100 said simply:

Protect our queer kids.

"That's us," Kai said, pointing to the sign.

"Us," Perry repeated.

I watched them staring at the sign like they might cry, like the old woman holding it might keel over before us. Their hands shook, like they'd been shaking at the bookstore and the Oddfellows Hall and I wondered, not for the first time, how much they'd been holding in.

Kai pulled out his phone and Aspen moved next to me to take my hand on one side, and Perry's on the other. Sage curled into their other side. And someone, I think it was Anna Baxter from the bank, started to clap and stomp. And someone else joined in.

My parents were there—I heard my dad's voice over the crowd as he stomped and cheered, and the sound echoed off the walls of the building and ricocheted around the parking lot.

The trucks kept revving behind us, but someone started chanting. "Kindness is stronger."

"Kindness is stronger."

And someone else joined in and then someone else and I yanked my hands from my friends and cupped them around my mouth and shouted at the top of my lungs. "Kindness is stronger."

Someone honked but we shouted and screamed, and more and more people filed into the parking lot, yelling from their car windows, dogs barking from backseats, little kids hollering and waving signs.

"Kindness is stronger."

Perry's moms. Mr. Bert.

The hockey team.

The florist. That guy with all the chickens that keep escaping.

And then the RCMP showed up and two officers got out. "Kindness is stronger," one of them yelled.

The trucks peeled out around the scores of cars and vans and motorcycles still pouring into the parking lot, parking along the street, on people's lawns, in the middle of the road. One of them threw a beer can but it landed in the gutter, and no one flinched.

When the last engine finally faded down Main Street, the town kept chanting and then we were laughing and hugging and someone started playing music and people brought coolers and at one point someone, I think it was Kai, said, "We're not going to school tomorrow," and all of our parents laughed.

Perry put their arms around me and leaned into me. "Do you think they'll be back?"

I pulled away for a minute and met their eyes. I wanted to say no. But I didn't know.

Instead, I held them tighter and said the only thing I knew was the truth. "If they do, I will, too."

Finnian Burnett *writes to explore the intersections of mental health, gender identity, and disability. Their work has appeared on* CBC Books, Blank Spaces Magazine, Pulp Literature, *and more. Finnian's novella-in-flash,* The Price of Cookies, *is available from* Off Topic Publishing. *When not teaching or writing, Finnian watches too much* Star Trek *and accidentally kills houseplants.*

Carousel

GLENNA TURNBULL

Funny to be scared of something the size of a popsicle stick. But it's not like I'm a little kid anymore or know ahead of time as I fumble with the wrapper whether it will be tropical pink or grape hiding inside. And instead of sticking this into my mouth, I'm about to pee on it.

Inside the McDonald's washroom, the smell of greasy fries and burgers mingle with some old lady who has the shits in the next stall. I put my chocolate shake on top of the toilet paper dispenser and my stomach starts gurgling. I try to ignore it as I lean forward to read the instructions again. It's really not that complicated: take the tester out of the tinfoil packaging, pee on it, then wait two minutes. I read it again anyway.

I stand up, grab my jeans by the loopholes and wriggle them down until they hug my knees. I hear my mother's voice inside my head, warning me like she used to at the mall, about the dreaded dangers of sitting on public toilets, so I try to squat and wrangle the stick into place but it's no good. I can't relax enough. So I plunk myself down onto the shiny germ-laden seat, exhale slowly, and aim the plastic stick into the streaming golden arch my body creates.

I'm pretty sure I already know the answer. I haven't had a period since Canada Day and my boobs feel like they're on fire, bursting out of the same bra that only weeks ago I denied stuffing.

I begin counting the one hundred and twenty seconds that will confirm whether or not I'm truly fucked.

Someone starts banging on the door. "Hey, there's a line out here!"

Another burst of diarrhea blasts into the porcelain bowl next door and as the smell wafts under the metal wall into my cubicle, the molten lava McDonald's shake in my belly comes bubbling up. As I jump to switch ends, my elbow smacks my drink cup and sends it flying. I shoot both hands up to grab my hair so I won't puke in it and accidentally drop the tester. I see it bounce off the rim but I'm too busy heaving out my Big Mac to notice where it lands.

Once my stomach is finally empty, I let go of my hair and wiggle my jeans back up. I glance down at the chocolate brown sludge pooled around my sneakers from the knocked down milkshake and that's when I see it: the little pink plus sign.

We're on our third lap around the building, no parking in sight. I scan the opposite side of the street so I don't have to read the signs held by privileged protesters who parade past the entrance. Mom puts on her four-way flashers and pulls into the handicap spot in front of the big glass hospital doors. She tells me to jump out quick. I agree there's really no reason for her to come inside. There'd been enough awkward small talk in the car yesterday when she'd taken me to the doctor's so he could stick something into my cervix to soften it. Besides, it's Uncle Dan's birthday and she needs to pick up the cake and the fresh seafood she's ordered for tonight's big family dinner. She says she'll come back for me when it's over. I wish John had a car. Or had offered to come with me on the bus. But I understand why he didn't want to drive here with my mom this early in the morning.

The nurse at check-in hands me a big white bag and two denim-coloured gowns, then says to remove everything.

"Put it on with the ties at the back."

She doesn't make eye contact—or maybe it's me who doesn't.

I'm in a ward with a bunch of older women who don't make eye contact either. My clothes fall in a heap beside my bed and I concentrate on how cold the floor feels under my bare feet as my hands shake, trying to form the strings into bows behind me.

"You need to take off that ankle bracelet," the nurse snaps, pointing to the one I'd made with John the first afternoon he asked me to hang out. He said the big bead in the middle looked like an eyeball and watched as I wrapped strands of jute around each other, entwining them like limbs, securing the glass orb into place. But now, my fingers falter like geeks in a gym class and the slipknots won't slip. I decide to leave it on, hoping the nurse won't notice.

But she does.

"Why do I have to take it off? It's on my fucking ankle!"

She flinches when I say 'fucking' and does not answer, just hands me a pair of orange handled scissors like the kind Mom buys in bulk from the dollar store. I part the legs of the blades wide enough for the hemp cord to slide in between them but the rope is tough and the edges are dull. I saw back and forth, over and over, that blue eyeball in the middle staring back at me, unblinking. I shred and shred until, rubbed raw, the strings finally break and the big bead drops to the floor. I throw the broken anklet at the wall as hard as I can. I drop the scissors and they clang onto the metal bedside table. I look over at the nurse. Then I make eye contact. I hold it. Tight.

I went online last night to research abortions, wanting to know if it was going to hurt. My friend Jodie has had one. She said it wasn't too bad but didn't want to talk about it. So I punched it into my computer but somehow got tricked into clicking a wrong link—a *very* wrong link because all of sudden, there splayed across my laptop screen, was a picture of something nobody should ever have to see. I tried to look away from the bloodied mess but couldn't. Then I started reading the details, written to create the maximum amount of guilt possible, preaching about this thing growing inside of me...using words like eyes...ears ... arms ... a beating... Fuck! I slammed my computer shut but the image would not go away. It just kept burning itself deeper and deeper into my mind.

I'm the kind of person who cries when I hear the mousetraps Dad sets at the cabin go off. I went into the kitchen one morning, before he'd had time to clean up the mess and ever since, any time I hear that spring snap, I'll lie there picturing the little mouse with its squished body and guts spilling out of its mouth. I still scream when I see one scuttle by, and I still hate them and want to be rid of them, but once I'd seen how the traps worked, it became hard to forget.

This was worse.

I know my school has a teen mom program but last night when I brought it up, Mom said keeping the baby was not an option. Everyone's told me, at sixteen, there's only one smart choice. Mom said I'm lucky we're Canadian, that I have a choice, that abortions are legal here and so much safer than when she was my age or when my Nana was growing up. She reminded me how hard the past few generations fought for this right, about the struggle going on in America right now, and what a mess I'd make of my life if I didn't do it.

"And don't think for one second that John will stick around," she said.

I bet it's a boy.

I studied John's face at the Toronto Exhibition Fair last weekend. On our way to the roller-coaster we passed through the kids' rides section. We stopped in front of the carousel and watched as the small children paraded past us, the confirmed results from McDonald's still sinking in. I pointed to the young boy in the bright red shirt with dark curly hair and big brown eyes like John's and said, "I bet that's what our baby would look like."

For a few minutes we talked about what we'd do if we could keep it. "I like the name Damien," he said, as the red-shirted boy on the silver plastic pony galloped by.

But the ride stopped, and when it started again, the curly haired kid was gone. John explained how his last two girlfriends got through their abortions just fine. "Don't worry, you'll be fine," he'd said.

"You'll wake up and it will all be over," Mom reassured me before dumping me at the door, "and you'll bounce right back. Dr. Lewis says the procedure has about the same impact on your body as having a tooth pulled."

I try holding onto these thoughts, but it doesn't help. What if John secretly wants me to keep it? Will he hate me later? I need to hear his voice but don't want all these nosey women listening.

I ask the nurse where the bathroom is and she looks up from her tablet and points with her stylus. "End of the hallway. Left after the nursing station. You might want to put on that second gown as a housecoat."

I glare back at her and bend over more than I need to pluck my phone out of my purse. I stride down the hallway, close the bathroom door, and call John. I hold my breath as it starts to ring. And ring. And ring. It goes to voicemail.

Fuck.

I call back two more times and finally, he answers.

"'h'llllllllo?"

"John?"

"Wwwhat time is it? Is it done?"

"Fuck you!"

I hang up and turn off my phone. I refuse to let the fact that he can sleep through this break me and I wiggle my bare ass in the most exaggerated manner possible as I strut past the bitchy nurse. I'm almost back to my assigned bed when my foot slaps down hard on something and I stumble. It's the big bead from my anklet.

"You might want to clean up your mess."

I glare back at her, then bend over to give her one more ass shot as I grab the bead, the limp remains of my severed anklet, and my pile of clothes, shoving everything into the big white plastic bag. I climb onto my bed and glance over at her, ready to burn her with my stare but she's not looking anymore.

I place my hands protectively across my belly, close my eyes and begin whispering my final farewell to Damien.

The orderly arrives to wheel me down to the elevator. I stare up at the fluorescent bulbs and watch as they begin to ripple like scales of shiny fish swimming downstream. I think of the signposts looping around and around outside the hospital, clasped in the hands of smug white men and privileged women, preaching the same facts I'd been tricked into reading online, making it clear in my brain the enormity of what I'm about to do.

Like the mice at the cottage. Snap. Done. Problem solved.

Goodbye little mouse...

I think of all the beach parties this summer—the beer and tequila shooters, the vaping, the Molly, the cigarettes and joints I've smoked. Maybe this little thing never stood a chance.

* * *

We lay in our beds lined up like naughty children outside the principal's office who'd been caught smoking, all of us not-wanna-be mothers who just went and got ourselves pregnant, waiting to be ushered in one by one through the operating room doors. I can't stop shivering. There is no warmth underneath this starchy sheet and thin blue gown, the chilled air heavy with the sterile smell of antiseptics. I can hear that I'm not the only one crying.

Finally, they come for me and I feel the wheels beneath my bed turning as we round the corner and push through the doors. I think of the pink plus sign drowning in the chocolate shake that had stared up at me from the McDonald's floor and all the arguments since. I think of the carousel and how Damien is here riding on this hospital gurney with me, but knowing that like the boy in the red shirt at the fair, after this metal horse stops, he will be gone when I come back around again.

My feet won't stop shaking as the doctor places them into the stirrups and pulls over the cannula pump, designed to suck out a fetus as efficiently as my mother's vacuum snatches up the mouse turds hidden on the floor beneath the refrigerator.

"Okay, try to relax while I insert the speculum."

I feel the cold stainless steel trying to wedge me open and suddenly, I don't know what takes over me but I jump back, push myself up off the table and scurry to the door. I kick it open and I run. I run and I run, my butt cheeks flashing out the back. I sprint to the end of the hallway and find a fire escape. Up the stairs I bolt, scaling two at a time. I slam through the heavy doors into another hallway and streak down it as well, almost laughing when I rush past two old men in wheelchairs, watching the sudden erection of their spines as I pass. I find another stairwell and keep climbing up up up. I tell Damien his mother is fucking crazy as I curl myself into a ball and hug my knees at the very top. I imagine my mother's voice telling me not to sit with my privates touching the dirty floor and clamp my hands over my ears to shut her out.

I'm not sure how long I've been hiding when she finds me.

"You don't have to go through with this, you know."

It's the bitchy nurse from the ward. I am not expecting this sort of kindness from anyone, especially not her, and suddenly all of the stress from the past few weeks come flooding out as she holds me in her arms and lets me cry, telling me that there are no easy answers, only choices.

She leads me back to the operating room so the doctor can remove the softening plug from my cervix. I cannot stop shaking. All I want is more time to think but he says I'm already twelve weeks along, that it's now or never.

One by one, the other women are wheeled back into the ward and the nurse brings us all apple juice and cookies. My mother arrives, looking sympathetic until she learns what I've done. Then her nostrils flare as she fumbles for words, but all she can spit out is, "How could you do this? You have no idea..."

I watch as she turns on her heel and marches ahead of me past the nursing station, down the hallway and out to the pay parking lot. I climb in beside Uncle Dan's cake. Its syrupy smell has mingled with the bag of shrimp in the backseat and within seconds, the apple juice and cookies hit reverse before my mother can.

I will phone John when I get home. Maybe he'll be happy when I tell him we're going to be parents, how one day we can take Damien with us to the fair.

I reach into my bag and pull out the giant bead I'd reclaimed from the floor. I roll it around and around in my palm as we drive home in silence, its big blue eye boring deeper into me at every turn.

Glenna Turnbull's short fiction has appeared in Best Canadian Stories 2025, Prism International, Room, The New Quarterly and Riddle Fence *here in Canada along with some US literary journals as well. Her debut novel is forthcoming with Breakwater Books in early 2026.*

Third Shift

ROBERT RUNTÉ

Ravi had just worked a double shift and was having trouble keeping his eyes open. He had nevertheless valiantly taken charge of baby Mina, thrust into his arms before he had even opened the door to his home. He knew his wife must be as exhausted as he, and undoubtedly more stressed by the endless squalling he had escaped while at work. Tired as he was, he had no choice but to take his turn.

Now, he was questioning that decision. He had already been startled awake by the sound of tires on rumble strips as he'd drifted out of his lane into oncoming traffic. Fortunately, this late at night, traffic was scarce, and he'd been able to get back into his own lane without incident. Nevertheless, falling asleep at the wheel—even momentarily—was terrifying.

The adrenaline rush of that scare had re-energized him sufficiently he judged it safe to continue driving, at least until Mina finally drifted off.

Mina settled down to a quiet whimpering, indicative that sleep might, at last, be approaching, but her wailing had actually been helping him stay awake. In the silence and the uninterrupted dark of their long drive, he recognized he was putting both their lives—and possibly those of a carload of strangers—at risk.

And then, ahead in the distance, he spotted the familiar sign of a 24-hour Tim Horton's. What he desperately needed for the now hour-long return trip home, was a steady supply of caffeine. An extra-large double-double with a side of Timbits might well see him and Mina safely home.

As he drove into the Tim's parking lot, he realized it was one of the older locations that didn't have a drive-thru. He pulled into the far corner of the lot, deeply disappointed. He needed that coffee. It probably wasn't safe for him to proceed without caffeine. But there was no way he could carry Mina's car seat into a noisy Tim's without her waking up.

Okay, then. Option 1 was to have a quick nap in the front seat to take the edge off. But slumped in a van at the edge of a Tim's parking lot at two a.m. could look suspiciously like someone awaiting a drug deal. Ravi knew from previous experience that his was a face cops loved to profile. He glanced at himself in the rear-view mirror and recognized that his four-day's growth of beard was not helpful. He looked positively ragged.

Slightly annoyed that he'd let himself go like this, he had to admit that this past week had been rough. He'd been more or less coping with Mina's sleeplessness and Claire's grumpiness, but then the Eastside plant had gone offline, forcing his crew to take on a second shift. Personal grooming had taken a backseat to maximizing sleep while still getting back in time for the regular morning shift. Everybody had come into work this week looking like they'd been through the wars.

Ravi looked longingly at the brightly lit windows of the Tim's. There were a dozen customers scattered among the tables and two guys working behind the long display cases of donuts.

He glanced back at Mina and considered Option 2. She was definitely asleep now. He could probably get out and close the door without waking her. He could run over to the Tim's, grab his extra-large double-double and Timbits and be back in the van in under three minutes. Parked way over here, no one in the Tim's would be able to spot Mina in the backseat. If he approached the Tim's from the far side, as if he'd come in on the sidewalk, he could even make it look he'd arrived on foot.

Ravi sighed. After the Walmart incident, Claire had made

it exceedingly clear what she would do to him if he ever again left Mina alone in a vehicle. It hadn't mattered that it had only been a few minutes before he'd realized what he'd done and gone back for the baby. He'd been so tired. Running into the Westgate Walmart to quickly grab something was so habitual and having a baby so new, he'd forgotten, just for a moment, that she was asleep there in the back. It was long enough, though, for some busybody to phone the cops on him. Fortunately, he'd gotten back to the van before they'd arrived, but they'd still given him the full, extended lecture on baby safety. He must have failed to hide his impatience because the woman officer had stopped mid-sentence. Clearly annoyed, she had insisted instead on his phoning Claire to confess the lapse to her. He wasn't convinced they legally had the authority to make him do that, but he'd had enough previous experience with the police to know better than to argue.

So that had been a low point of married life. Claire had not let go of it in the months since. Though maybe tonight's handing off of Mina could be taken as a sign Claire was relenting a little. That, or how far-gone Claire herself had been that she had chosen to trust him rather than her own ability to endure Mina's crying a single minute longer.

"I wouldn't cry all the time if you were better parents," Mina said.

Or hadn't said, Ravi realized, jerking awake. He rubbed

his eyes. "We'd be better parents if you were prepared to sleep anywhere besides the van," Ravi told her softly. He turned back to stare at the beaconing brightness of the Tim's.

He was starting to close the cab door before he registered that he'd made his decision. Only at the very last second did he realize his mistake and jerk the door open again before it could click locked.

Taking a deep breath, he reached back inside to yank his jacket over from the passenger seat and fish out his key fob. He closed the door, then leaned against it imagining the consequences had he actually locked himself out, with Mina still inside.

Gathering himself, he pulled his phone out of his back pocket and set the timer. *Three minutes*, he promised. He turned and jogged off toward the sidewalk that would take him into Tim's. He was through the door and to the counter as the person ahead of him was finishing up their order. He glanced down at the timer: 2:18 left.

"I'll have an extra-large, double-double," Ravi said, "And six Timbits, chocolate glazed."

The clerk plucked six Timbits out of the display case with his tongs, dropped the half-sized paper bag on the counter, and turned his back on Ravi to walk to the coffee machine.

Timer: 2:01.

"About five minutes," the clerk announced. "I'll have to start a new batch for you. This has been sitting too long."

"No, no!" Ravi cried, not quite shouting. "It's fine."

The clerk looked dubious. "I'm not supposed to serve it after it's been sitting. Twenty minutes, max."

"It's fine, "Ravi repeated. "I, uh, prefer it old. Strong. Steeped. I'll take it. As is."

Timer: 1:44.

The clerk shrugged and pulled an extra-large cup off the end stack.

Ravi let out a breath, having dodged that bullet. He reached for his debit card.

Shit! Another shot of adrenaline as he patted his pockets, realizing he'd left his wallet and cards in his jacket, back in the van.

Timer: 1:34.

The clerk plucked the coffee down in front of Ravi, fitted on the lid. "What's wrong?"

"Sorry, sorry. I've forgotten my wallet." Ravi fished frantically for change in his pants pocket. "What can I get for"—he glanced at his find—"a loonie and two dimes?"

The clerk straightened and looked Ravi carefully up and down. "No, it's okay. It's on me."

"What?"

"On the house. It was old coffee anyway. I was going to throw it out." He pushed the coins back at Ravi. "And the Timbits are on me."

"What?"

The clerk leaned across the counter to whisper. "I know what it's like. I was on the street a couple years myself, before I got a break. Pay it forward when you get the chance."

"No, you don't understand. I just left my wallet in the van," Ravi said, pointing with his thumb in the general direction of the parking lot.

"Yeah, I used to 'forgot my wallet' all the time, too. I understand, really. It's tough being a refugee."

"What? I'm not—" Ravi glanced at his phone: 0:50. "Right." He gathered up his coins. "Thanks! God bless!"

Ravi pounded back to the van, chased by humiliation, and was in his seat with nine seconds to spare. Deep breath, quick check on sleeping Mina, cautious sip of overheated coffee, Timbit inserted and chewed, Ravi put the truck in gear.

As he drove out of the lot, Ravi committed to three resolutions. First, he could never return to this Tim's location. Second, he would buy a fifty-dollar Tim's gift card next time he was in some other Tim's and hand that to the first homeless guy he came across. Third, he would never, ever leave the house again without first taking time to shower and shave.

He took another sip of sweet-sweet coffee and turned on the radio low enough not to wake Mina, but tuned to an all-talk station guaranteed to keep him angrily awake and engaged for the journey home.

Robert Runté is Senior Editor with EssentialEdits.ca. A former professor, he has won three Aurora Awards for his literary criticism and currently reviews for the Ottawa Review of Books. His own fiction has been published over 100 times. Robert lives in Lethbridge, Alberta, with his wife, two daughters, and four dogs.

Allie & Fergus

C.A. O'BRIEN

From the age of three we were taught to tell people that fraternal twins came from two separate eggs, just like any other brother and sister, when people asked us why we didn't look alike.

At the age of six, our parents died in a car crash and we were placed in foster care.

By the age of seven, we were adopted into a new family who lived in small town just north of Toronto. It took a little longer than usual, because not many people wanted to take on two kids – or so we were told. Nor, did young parents want older kids. They wanted babies. Thankfully, they wanted to keep us together.

Back in the 80s, Fergus and I were still an anomaly. Mix-raced families were stared at, and we were asked absurd questions, like, "Is she your mom?" When we were born, my white mom asked her mother-in-law why our hair was straight and what the bruise-like markings were on our buttocks. I guess that's normal, as there are any number of genetic factors that go into making each and every one of us, and there are cultural differences. But, it's out of our hands, and that of our parents. It's a crap shoot. Someone decided that there were four major races in the world, which defines a group of people with common inherited features – Caucasian, Mongoloid, Negroid and Australoid. Who the fuck cares? Apparently, there are approximately four hundred breeds of dogs, but the long-nose Collie is just as revered as the flat-faced Pug. I was darker than Fergus and taller at the age of seven. My height overshadowed his until he had a major growth spurt at the age of fourteen. Everyone always thought that I was older, even though he slipped out first, making way for me, who was two pounds larger.

Little Fergus, as everyone still referred to him, had a beautiful mocha shade of skin, and soft curls. I was bequeathed a head of frizzy strands that had a mind of their own. A wild head of hair, so much hair, that taming it became a daily chore until I decided to shave it all off at the age of fifteen. I didn't take it right down to my scalp, just a close-cropped look. It suited me.

When we entered this new family, we were separated for the first time in our lives. It wasn't anything major, we were only a room apart, but our new caregivers decided that it was best if I slept with Joelle, who was a year younger than me, and that Fergus bunked in with Cole, who was eight.

In our first family, our mom was white and our father was black. In this family, it was reversed. There were times when I would see the tail end of one of them rounding a corner, and my mind would get mixed up and I wasn't sure who to call for.

The dad-like figure, for it was a long time before we would think of them as parents, hated to say more than one syllable, if he could help it. He'd call out, "Jo, Al, Ferg, Cole. Time for din. Come. Down. Now."

The adopted mother still carried her Jamaican accent like a heart-shaped locket against her chest. To my ear, her lyrical speech projected high notes and low notes in areas that seemed to be reversed. I mixed up questions and statements at times, and it took me a while to familiarize myself with her tonal inflections. She could braid my hair and do cornrows, so much softer than my white mom. It was as if she was plaiting a complex work of art, her fingers following an inherent pattern, while she hummed to herself. Though the finished project was well-crafted, it never felt right. Nothing seemed to go with my facial features, or so I thought. My limbs grew so fast that I wasn't sure of their length, and someone once said that I walked like a gangly bird. What sticks with us can always be traced back to what other people say. That gummy residue of a negative comment creates a film of shame, and can actually make you feel dirty. For, wasn't that the reason that people of colour couldn't swim, eat or sit with white people? We were less-than clean—not pure as the driven snow.

Joelle and Cole were a shade, or two, lighter than I was. I often pictured a scale of pigment samples, similar to paint chips, lined up in front of us when our photo was taken. Or maybe like one of those tooth-whitening kits that go from a yellowish, coffee-stained shade to a movie-star white. There might be a day when we can choose the desired tonal value of a mixed-race child, as well as their hair texture. People thought that they could govern the resulting gender identification of an infant for centuries. So, as more cultures mix and mingle, why not send waves of genetic signals into a womb to help to determine the final outcome? Few of us are ever satisfied with all of the components of our physical image, anyways. Knowing that a couple could actually choose the preferred physical traits of their offspring would certainly add fuel to a teenager's angst, and intensify the adolescent battleground against their know-nothing parents. How could you? Why did you make me look like this?

Life eventually imitated a family-like unit for us, and from the outside, we all seemed well-adjusted, well-kept and well-mannered. Friends were always dropping by for Cole, Joelle or myself, but I worried about Fergus. He was malleable, and would shapeshift his whole physical being, as well as his persona, in order to be in line with someone else's mindset. I could actually see him transform. So much so that I'd take him aside later and question him about it. "What the hell? You don't believe that." He'd shrug and tell me that it was just easier that way. "But I know that you don't agree with what they said. Stand up for yourself."

"I don't care to engage. So, I just go along."

I worried. I fretted. And I wasn't sure if anyone else was noticing. Even at home, he'd roll over like a loveable puppy, let mom or dad tickle his fancy, and respond with a nod and a giggle. How could you not love this easy-going character? He never gave anyone a minute of worry. Except for me.

As far as sisters go, Joelle mimicked everything that I did, and while slightly annoying, I took to her like a bee to honey. She was very sweet, and I could see that, with me, she had an advantage with her own at-odds appearance as she watched me navigate the white trails, even when I side-stepped, took a wrong turn or decided to go in a different direction.

Fergus and Cole were only a year apart, but to see them together was like witnessing the tortoise and the hare in a race. You knew that they were of the same species, but their stature, their movements and mannerisms were so different that they appeared to be disparate organisms. They got along quite well, but Fergus spent more time in their room, than Cole.

I think most young girls like the idea of having an older brother, especially when their friends come around. It was like having a built-in view finder, where I'd squint and alter the frame as I sat demurely on the front porch assessing their attributes. It didn't just go one way. I could fantasize as well.

Single syllable 'pop' was named Anthony. Shortening it to Tony proved to be too long for him, so everyone called him Ton. And mom Rodelle was Ro. Ton and Ro were in the throes of planning a surprise sixteenth birthday party for

Fergus and I, but the wind carried whispers of this upcoming event from day one. Cole and Joelle were recruited to help with the guest list, and it was during these preparations that everyone realized that no one really knew any of Fergus's friends, except for Bren. But was Bren short for Brenda or Brennen? I knew of course, but I wasn't supposed to know about the party. I looked up the name 'Brennen' one day and found out that it came from the Irish word 'braon', which translates to 'sorrow' or 'teardrop', reminding the baby that sadness is a natural, healthy emotion. It seemed to suit Brennen to a 'T'.

Ton didn't like to waste time. He'd try to find the shortest way to get to his destination, make note of his drive time, and then try to beat it on his return trip. Even when cooking, he'd skip a step or two, for efficiency's sake, but then he'd be disappointed when his dish didn't even resemble the photo in the cook book. However, I give him credit when it came to us kids. He didn't consider us to be time wasters. If there was an issue to be discussed, he'd sit us down and give us his full attention. He didn't spare words in these situations. If anything, he'd parrot quotes from books, explain his point of view in detail and leave our heads swirling with more information than we had bargained for. He didn't talk down to us. He asked us insightful questions that helped us to determine the right approach for ourselves. But if you didn't take a ladle and stir the pot now and then, then these one-on-ones stewed in your brain for days to come. We didn't view these intense talks as punishment, but they were usually reserved for serious matters. Mama Ro handled more of the day-to-day challenges of messy rooms, uncompleted chores and sibling squabbles. With four kids she was constantly reshuffling schedules and dealing out a new deck of cards at every turn. It was often difficult to keep up with her, and we didn't always know when to play our hand. We'd watch her for any signs of a slip-up, but she was an ace organizer and a queen at multi-tasking. She'd get completely exasperated now and then. So much so, that we'd all stop in our tracks, wide-eyed and willing to do whatever she asked of us. In the next moment, she'd be laughing at something that she did, and again we'd check in with each other with a sideways glance to see if it was okay to join in. And, it was. She didn't hold grudges, and once she dealt with an issue, it was time to move on.

I decided to go to Cole, and admit to him that I knew about the party plans. He and I shared a brother, but my twin bond superseded any male bonding that they might have experienced. As for the two of us, it was rare that we were ever in the same space at the same time. And, if we were, other family members were present. I was nervous. At seventeen, Cole was a star athlete and received lots of attention from girls. He had a smile that melted heart after heart and left puddles of desperation behind him. Any direct attention from this caramel-coloured stallion broke even the most dogged fillies. I related this horse metaphor to him one day after witnessing one of the popular girls fall completely out of grace, because he complimented her on her earrings.

He roared with laughter and I experienced that same heart-wrenching squeeze that left me breathless. We lived together as brother and sister, but we weren't related.

I was sitting beside him on a bench in the park at the end of our street to talk about Fergus. I didn't want to be across a table from him in a coffee shop, because I didn't want to be distracted. "I don't think this party is a good idea."

"I agree," he said. "But mom won't listen. Even Ton is caught up in the whole sweet sixteen thing. Geesh, last year for my sixteenth the six of us went to Swiss Chalet." At this point he laughed. "I think, for them," he went on. "It's like a rite of passage into our family. Not to say that you're not family, just that we've hit a milestone as teenagers. And, who knows how long we'll all be living at home?"

"It's a wonderful gesture. I'm just worried about Fergus. He doesn't like to be the centre of attention, at the best of times." I was going to add, 'like you', but my brain reconsidered the words, and I bit my tongue a little too hard before they could come out. The sting reminded me of when I burnt my tongue after taking a sip of a really hot Hot Chocolate. It lasted for days. The two us sat quietly for a couple of minutes considering the alternatives.

I think," we both said at the same time.

"You first," I nodded.

"Let's just be straight with them," and he turned his head to look at me – those deep dark eyes penetrating my soul. Again, I only nodded because I couldn't talk. "I'll tell mom and dad that someone spilled the beans and that you're concerned about Fergus."

"How will you explain my concern?"

"That you think that Fergus would be self-conscious and uncomfortable." Then he added. "What if I suggest that we have a family dinner at home, and each of us gets to bring a friend? Since it's your birthday, you and Fergus get to pick the menu – your favourite dishes."

"I think it's perfect." Cole's grin widened and my arms went weak.

"I think Fergus will choose Mama Ro's rice and peas with curried chicken, but we'll ask him for sure. As for me, I'm tempted to ask Ton to make that Thai curry he made a couple of weeks ago, as long as he promises to follow the recipe."

"Two different types of curries?" His laugh bubbled up to a warm, thick gravy that coated the goose bumps on my skin, and I was grateful that my legs didn't have to support me at that moment.

The celebratory evening arrived. Joelle had gone all out with balloons and decorations, and Mama Ro had put two tables together to seat the ten of us. The aroma of simmering pots was mouth-watering, and two cakes sat on the sideboard – chocolate for Fergus and vanilla for me. I had invited my best friend, Jules. As I stood back, I was able to witness the scene for what it was. Fergus's guest was the last to arrive and once he introduced him to everyone, it was Ton, not Mama Ro, who asked him if he preferred to be called Bren or Brennen.

C.A. O'Brien *has been a professional writer and editor (byline: Catherine Daley) for more than four decades, contributing to major newspapers and periodicals, as well as editing a series of magazines for a well-known publishing company. Two books by C.A. O'Brien are now available:* Negative Spaces *and* Conclusion: A Fictional Ending to a Somewhat True Story. *Her website is caobrien.ca*

The Hockey Game

MURGATROYD MONAGHAN

R ob took attendance as a matter of protocol.

"Charlie?"

"Hee-ya!" Charlie never made any attempt to conceal his accent. In fact, he seemed to accentuate it wildly on purpose, like English was a game. To top it all off, Charlie seemed terribly happy today. This annoyed everyone but Rob.

"Maria?"

"Here."

"Saeed?"

"Here."

"Mbana?"

"Yes?" The others chuckled, and Mbana flushed. She was always serious, but often distracted. "I apologize. I am here".

Rob's Leafs jersey flapped hard as the subway train approached with a loud gust of air. He was so excited that he had checked everyone's name off before they had responded, and the clipboard was already back inside his satchel. He raised his voice loudly to be heard over the sound of the subway train pulling into the station. "Now, this is my favourite part of teaching English to you newcomers, you understand, and it's the most important – probably the absolute most important – thing you'll do as a new Canadian. Consider this just as important as your citizenship ceremony, okay?"

Saeed tapped Maria, grinning. "We are going to have to listen to this man all night."

Maria shook her head, amused. "He is a small child at *carnaval*. And to think, the staff is watching my little children at the school for this."

The doors chimed their opening sound, and Rob repeated each name hurriedly as he touched each one of their shoulders and whisked them inside. "Charlie, Saeed, Maria, Mbana, okay, that's it, go, go, get in!" The doors chimed their tritone sound and closed hard onto Rob, as he squeezed enthusiastically into the remaining space behind the closing doors.

"Now, I want you guys to look at this map," Rob said, pointing. "We are here, where the light is green, see? This is College station." He sounded the word out slowly as he moved his index finder across it. "We are going," he pointed out each dot as he said the name, "Dundas, Queen, King, Union. Four stops." He held up four fingers.

"One, two, three, four," chimed Charlie sycophantically. Maria rolled her eyes.

Rob sighed. "It wouldn't kill you to try, Maria."

It wouldn't kill her. How easily people told this lie here. Maria wondered if Rob had ever seriously feared death at all. It made it hard to take anything he said seriously. She looked sideways at Saeed. He was slouching beside her and looking at his feet. Mbana was staring straight ahead and holding onto the pole with two hands as though her mission was extremely serious and her vessel was about to tip at any moment. Charlie had a grin on his face as wide as the ocean.

Exiting the subway at Union station was a formidable feat. Saeed kept his eyes on the little trinkets hanging from Rob's backpack. One was a pot-bellied doll with green hair. Another was a flashlight. Yet another was a religious icon, a cross, like the white missionaries used to have on their clothes and their buildings back home. He hadn't seen those since he was a teenager, before the coup. He'd had a white friend, a son of a missionary couple, and they had played football together. David—that was his name. It was funny to remember David in a busy place such as this. Usually, thoughts of David came to him only when he was alone. Perhaps it was the thought of sport that gave him the association, he thought. He squeezed his nails into his palms, willing the wrong thoughts to go away. He hoped David had grown into a happy man, Inshallah. That was all.

Mbana never had trouble following Rob. She did so quietly, with military submission. Maria too, could keep her eye on a man in a crowd without any difficulty. Charlie's face took in so many sights that their whole group was slowed more than once. It was a wonder Rob didn't need to hold his hand.

Emerging from the underground into the open, the sun had almost fallen below the skyline and the air was crisp and thin. Charlie put on mittens, a scarf, a balaclava, and a hat. He put the mittens on first, so that to watch him put the other items on was tedious and embarrassing. He still had his coat to zip up. Maria couldn't take it anymore. She snapped her fingers and pointed at the space in front of her. "*Aqui.*" She looked at Rob apologetically. "Here. Be here. I will do." Maria zipped Charlie's puffy coat for him all the way to his mouth.

"Like a Canadian," came Charlie's muffled voice, proudly.

"Yes, all the Canadians who are in only shirts and *pantalones*. I see them." Maria swept her arm wide. She wasn't unkind. Only efficient, and well-practiced at sarcasm.

Rob made a face that said he didn't agree. Though he was in basketball shorts and a jersey, he had now placed a Leafs toque on his head, and he pointed it out to Charlie and Maria with a wink that made Maria groan, and Charlie beam.

"Spare a little change?" A man had wandered up to them shaking a weathered Tim Horton's cup containing coins. Charlie froze, looking at Rob for a reaction. Maria looked away awkwardly. Saeed was opening his mouth for something to say, when he saw Mbana's hand returning to her pocket. A ten-dollar bill was in the man's hand. The man wandered off to the next group to ask for more change.

Saeed's eyes were wide. "He didn't even thank you." Mbana shrugged. She was unreadable, and serious as ever.

Rob acknowledged the teachable moment. "That was very nice of you, Mbana. But you don't have to give those people money, you know. Like I mean, don't feel like you have to. They can be pushy. But don't let it get to you."

Let it get to her? Pushy men did not get to her. No, it was the women. Mbana had crossed the ocean to avoid the pushy women. Stony-faced but alert, her eyes blurred and her shins weakened as she remembered her sister's screams as their mother and aunties had held her sister down to be cut. It was female tradition, they had told her. To be a woman, her sister had to be cut, or else she would be killed. It was Mbana who had tricked her older sister that day. She had obediently told her sister to go in the house, knowing what awaited her. It was Mbana who had held her sister's head to stop her from escaping. Her sister's blood was on now Mbana's hands. What could ten dollars ever buy her? Absolution? No. Freedom? Never. It was just money. The women in her family had said her sister died only because she resisted. But Mbana remembered the blood. There was so much blood running from the wound between her sister's legs that it seemed to fill the ocean she'd crossed, just to make it all the way into her nose and mouth and belly and choke her.

"You good?" Rob wanted to know. Mbana just shrugged again.

As they walked into the Air Canada Centre, everyone in their motley ensemble was silent. The sounds were deafening and a variety of thick smells permeated the gut. Between Charlie's outrageous winter outfit, Maria's sarcastic outburst, Mbana's outlandish handout, and Saeed's intrusive thoughts, there was a distinct air of annoyance.

Rob was in his own little fantasy world. "These tickets were a company donation. We're right up front. Can ya believe it? Can ya even believe it? This is the dream, guys. The dream. Pile in. Come on. Wow."

They sat. Rob handed out tickets to each person and they all traded until they were holding the ticket with their seat number on it. The way he was so excited about handing each ticket out, they almost thought he intended for them to frame it.

Rob pointed. "This here is where the goalie goes. We're gonna be right behind him, see? He's the one who stops the puck. The puck is—well, you know, it goes in the net."

"Puck is ball?" asked Saeed.

"No, no, not a ball. It's uh—well, like a ball, yeah, but it's flat." Rob made his hands into preposterous shapes trying to show this.

"Ah," said Saeed.

"You play any sports?" Rob asked Saeed, grateful for the potential interest.

"No. Well—yes. Long time ago. Football."

"Oh yeah. Football like football, or like soccer?"

"Sorry?"

"You know, like, is the ball pointy and brown and you throw it? Or is it round and black and white and you kick it?"

"Kick. Kick the football." Saeed kicked his foot to demonstrate.

"Oh, okay. Yeah, we call that soccer."

"Soccer?"

"Yeah. You any good? You play for your country or whatever?"

"Ha. Not that good. I don't like it really."

"No? Why'd you play, then?" Something in Saeed's faraway grin was universal enough to catch Rob's elbow in Saeed's rib. "Ohhh, I get it. A girl, eh?"

Saeed was still smiling at his feet. "Something like that." The thought of David made his knees weak, and he was glad he was sitting.

Maria was telling Charlie something about her children. He looked like a snowman, all wrapped up, with only his eyes visible. "You gonna stay like this?" She gestured at his face and the scarf wrapped around it.

"Is cold. Cold in hee-ah."

"Ay. *Si*. Cold is nice."

"You like cold?"

"I like to know I'm not going to cook, you know?"

Charlie laughed like she had made a funny joke. "Cook! Cook you. Cook Maria. So funny. So funny Maria."

Maria didn't laugh. Some of them had cooked. In the truck, coming across the border, at least ten of them. The old ones, the very young ones, and even a pregnant woman. There were more than fifty of them in that truck. Her two girls had survived, but barely. Now that her protected status was expiring in the States, she had done it again, crossed into Canada this time. One of her girls nearly didn't go. She had been so afraid, remembering the heat and the bodies. It was the description of snow that Maria had used to convince her and to soothe her fears. She smiled at the snow now, piled up around the rink. Something in her softened. "Hey, Charlie?"

"Yeah?"

"You like snow?"

"Oh yes! I love it. Love snow. I never actually touch snow, though. Never one time."

Maria got up wordlessly and put a finger to her lips for Charlie. He put his finger to his lips in return, like he was keeping her secret. Then she was gone.

Saeed couldn't tell if the music was louder, or the crowd. Finally, he decided that Rob was the loudest.

"You know this song, Saeed?"

"I don't know American music."

"Canadian. Canadian, Saeed. These guys are Rush. Huge Canadian band."

"Rush? Like hurry-hurry? What they sing about?"

"Oh, uh, life, you know. Love, freedom, art, that stuff."

"This is Canadian life? Love, freedom, art?"

"Yeah. And hockey. Here, look, they're gonna come out now."

The air went suddenly dark, and a spotlight played across the rink. Despite herself, Mbana sat on the edge of her seat, eyes glued to the light. Electric guitars whined like sirens and drums beat out high energy riffs like automatic weapons, but she found she was clenching the edge of her seat with excitement more than fear.

"Ladies and gentlemen, I give you, your . . . *Toronto Maple Leafs*!" A voice over the loudspeaker shouted this, though the last word was nearly drowned out by screaming. *Screaming.* There was screaming. No. Wait, where was Maria? Stupid, thought Mbana. Stupid, stupid. How could I have let myself get sucked into this? Someone has taken Maria. God forgive me, I have let another young woman be hurt. Mbana's throat contorted as she looked between the three men – Rob, Charlie, Saeed – who should she tell? Should she say anything? Perhaps Maria was getting away on purpose. Perhaps she knew what she was doing.

Feet ran up beside her in the dark, and Mbana sat deathly still. "Boo!" A snowball hit Mbana in the lap. Mbana just stared, shocked. "Ha!" A second snowball hit Charlie, square in the chest. Charlie's eyes sparkled with delight.

"My turn, my turn!" Charlie reached his arms out toward Maria. She had filled her whole purse with snow. Charlie made a snowball that promptly fell apart and threw the tiny clumps at Saeed.

Fear flashed in Saeed's face, then anger. "Ah! What is wrong with you, Charlie?" Saeed snapped.

Charlie stiffened. Did they know his secret? Had he been careless, the way his mother told him not to be when he walked with her that day in the market? *Our son is different*, Charlie had heard her tell his father in hushed tones that night, while Charlie slept. *He needs to be with my sister in Canada, so he can have a chance.*

Saeed squinted apologetically at Charlie's tearful expression. The anger had been less and less since Saeed had arrived, but it still happened, especially when something took him by surprise. He smiled softly and put an arm around Charlie. "Come on, bro. You have to make like ball. You know ball?"

Charlie exhaled with relief.

"Like football, you know? Or soccer. What it is. Anyway. See?" Saeed dipped his hands into Maria's purse and held a perfect sphere in his hands.

The four friends froze, the same mischievous idea filling the air between them. Four heads swiveled slowly towards Rob, who was watching the ice intently, totally oblivious. Charlie looked at Saeed devilishly and put his finger to his lips, like Maria had showed him. "You do it," Saeed said to Mbana. Saeed handed her the snowball, and she watched Rob, waiting for the opportune moment, wanting to get it right. Everything felt like an enormous weight.

But the snowball was so small, and cold, and smooth. It was not heavy at all, and it made her feel happy. Mbana seemed to hear her sister's voice cut clearly through the waves of sound and chaos. *Do it, cheli!* The effect was stunning, and Mbana gasped. Loosened by a sudden feeling of joy, she turned away from Rob and dropped the snowball down Saeed's shirt instead.

Saeed hopped up out of his seat. "Ayee!"

That was when Mbana began to laugh. She laughed, and laughed, and the sound alerted Rob, who had finally been pulled out of his trance.

"Woah, what's up with you?" he said, looking sideways at Mbana. Mbana grabbed a snowball from Maria, and lobbed it at him. Rob ducked.

"Ha! Yours are just as bad as Charlie's!" Saeed taunted. "Here." He made another ball. "This here, like *soccer* ball," he said, looking at Rob for approval.

"But this is hockey," said Charlie. "And this," he announced, extending his mitten triumphantly, "is *puck*." He squished Saeed's perfect snow sphere into a pancake.

"Hey!"

Maria emptied the last of the snow onto everyone's heads, laughing hysterically. "Woohoooo!"

"Who's at car-na-val now, Spanish girl?", mocked Saeed.

"Um, that's Canadian girl, *por favor*." Maria tipped up her chin and puffed out her chest like royalty.

The sounds of their laughter seemed to linger awkwardly as a sudden silence stopped up their ears. It was abrupt, as if the whole arena had been suddenly tossed overboard and plunged underwater. Twenty thousand people stood at once, like a wave. Rob removed his hat, then Charlie's. The hockey players had their hands across their chests.

It was the first time the arena had been quiet.

The first words of the anthem rang like a bell through the ocean of air. Everyone was stinging with cold where the snow had hit them, but no one spoke or moved. It felt like magic.

When the last note had faded from the air, Saeed didn't sit. He felt like crying with an overwhelming sense of belonging. He had never dared to wish so clearly that David could be holding his hand, but found that now he had allowed the wish to touch him, he couldn't stop thinking about it. "Rob? Which one was that?"

"Huh?"

"Was that one love, freedom, or art?"

Rob shook his head and handed Saeed a Coke. "It was hockey, man. Just hockey. The puck's about to drop. Come on."

Murgatroyd Monaghan is an Autistic mother, writer, poet and spoken word artist of mixed descent. Her work tells the stories of the diverse people of Turtle Island. When she isn't

writing or travelling, Murg can be found curled up on the couch watching Star Trek *with her three kiddos. Her poetry collection* white spaces where we learn to breathe *is forthcoming from Off Topic Publishing.*

Exodus into an Unknown Country

Fatmir Sadiku

Exodus to an Unknown Country

After a long journey from Skopje, the Boeing 777 touched down at Trenton Military Base. At the exit stairs, the captain and crew offered warm farewells, their well-wishes sincere, almost tender. As I stepped off the plane, I thanked them for their care and professionalism. A line of people stood waiting to greet us, their smiles radiating warmth and hope. One by one, immigration clerks, army officers, and Red Cross volunteers shook our hands and welcomed us to Canada, their voices steady and reassuring. A sudden wave of panic surged through me. My thoughts spiraled: *How would I navigate this vast, unfamiliar continent? Would my family be safe? What new trials lay ahead?* Canada, this land of promise, loomed large—full of opportunity, yet overwhelmingly unknown.

We were guided to a nearby hangar, where doctors in

spotless white coats waited to conduct medical examinations. Concerned about contamination, they firmly instructed us to leave all our possessions behind. It was necessary, yet deeply unsettling—as if we were shedding the last tangible pieces of our former lives.

In the next room, volunteers greeted us with kind eyes and gentle smiles. They handed out donated clothing— ordinary garments that, in that moment, felt like symbols of care. After the inspections, we were led to another building where a hot meal awaited. The meal was modest, but its warmth and thoughtful preparation spoke volumes. Volunteers moved gently among us, encouraging us to eat. Some knelt beside children, coaxing laughter with toys or quiet words, granting parents a rare moment to simply breathe.

Later that night, families were taken to hangars lined with mobile beds. Despite their efforts, the firm mattresses offered little comfort. My mind raced with fragments of our journey—border crossings, whispered prayers, hurried goodbyes—and unanswered questions about what lay ahead. Sleep hovered out of reach. But sometime around two in the morning, the weight of it all finally pulled me under. Weariness won where fear could not.

The next day began early, ushering us into a rigid routine of medical checkups and immigration interviews. From six in the morning until late at night, the process was meticulous, impersonal, and exhausting. By the second night, the hangars had emptied noticeably. From nearly three hundred people, only about thirty remained. Most had completed their processing and moved on to new homes. The silence in the hangar was striking, broken only by the occasional cry of a baby—each sound echoing louder in the emptiness, amplifying our sense of displacement.

Yet through it all, Canadian volunteers remained steady and kind. They played with children, shared quiet smiles, and helped us find brief moments of joy amid the blur of waiting. Even now, I don't remember everything that was said—but I remember how it felt. Kindness shown. Patience offered. The unspoken understanding that we were not just numbers or files, but people—tired, frightened, and full of hope. That first night, wrapped in a borrowed blanket, I realized something quietly powerful: we had lost so much, but we had also arrived. We were not yet home, but we were somewhere safe. Somewhere that offered the chance to begin again. And in that fragile in-between—between fear and possibility, loss and renewal—I found a flicker of something I hadn't felt in a long time. Not certainty, but maybe . . . the beginning of belonging.

On the third morning, just after nine o'clock, we were told to board the waiting bus. The coach—broad-shouldered and weatherworn—stood like a sentinel, ready to carry us forward. It would take us to Borden, a military base that, for a time, would be home.

As the bus rolled away, I turned to the window. Outside, the world unfurled in slow motion—vast stretches of dense forests and open fields, places untouched by time. By noon, we arrived. Borden greeted us with its neat rows of buildings and quiet discipline. We stepped off the bus and into the unknown, into a place that would shape us—perhaps even hold us—for the next chapter of our lives.

The Ministry of Immigration and the Red Cross moved

quickly into action, mobilizing resources and people. Volunteers poured in from every corner of the country, united not by obligation but by a profound desire to help. Among them were members of the Albanian community in Canada, whose presence was vital. They served as interpreters, bridging the language divide between aid workers and refugees, offering comfort with every translated word.

As grassroots efforts gained momentum, Canada launched Operation Parasol—an ambitious initiative that airlifted 5,000 refugees to safety. It wasn't just an act of evacuation; it was an embrace. Refugees were welcomed not only with shelter but with pathways to housing and language training—foundations for a future far from war. Alongside this, the Kosovo Family Reunification Program reconnected 2,200 people with loved ones torn apart by conflict. Each reunion re-ignited hope and reminded the world of what compassion in action can achieve.

Canada took further steps, offering refugee status to all Kosovars seeking peace. The Resettlement Assistance Program (RAP) became a lifeline, helping families stabilize during their first two years. Individual and organizational sponsors were key—helping newcomers enrol their children in school, open bank accounts, and access medical care.

To deepen this commitment, Canada introduced the Joint Assistance Sponsorship (JAS) program—a powerful collaboration between government and private sponsors. More than just resettlement, JAS offered integration. It helped bridge the distance from trauma to healing, from displacement to belonging. Refugees were given time to breathe, to recover, to reconnect—with themselves and with a supportive community.

Within days of our arrival, Prime Minister Jean Chrétien and his wife visited the camp. Their presence was more than symbolic—it was personal. They listened to stories, shared smiles, and even played basketball with young refugees, embodying the warmth and humanity of a nation standing in solidarity.

The media echoed this sentiment, broadcasting daily updates that captured the heart of the town of Angus, where compassion had become contagious. Through regular press releases, the Ministry of Immigration kept the public informed, reaffirming its commitment to the refugees.

Life in the Military Base

A week after we arrived at the base, the Red Cross, in collaboration with local educators, began organizing English language testing for refugees who wished to participate. The tests, ranging from beginner to advanced, helped place us at the appropriate learning levels. With limited space, classes were split into two shifts to keep them small and manageable.

Kabashi arrived shortly after, with his wife and two sons. A former teacher fluent in several languages, he quickly became a pillar of our community. With support from the Red Cross, he served as an interpreter—but his efforts extended far beyond that. He organized make-up classes for Albanian children who had missed months of school due to the war. Math, language, science—subjects once taken for granted— became tools of healing and hope. Supplies began to arrive: boxes of textbooks, notebooks, pencils, and art materials. They felt like lifelines in our fragile, temporary world. Still, there were gaps. Refugees stepped up to teach Albanian language and music, but no one had taken on history and geography.

I had spent thirteen years as a secondary school teacher. For me, teaching was never just a job—it was a calling. So, I offered to teach history and geography.

At first, we followed Kosovo's national curriculum. It was familiar and grounding. But as time passed, it became clear that many families—mine included—might remain in Canada. That realization stirred something in me. I proposed adding Canadian history and geography to our lessons, hoping to give the children a sense not only of where they'd come from, but where they were going. I translated sections of textbooks from English to Albanian, and with support from the Red Cross, we made the shift.

One of the most memorable moments from that time was a visit to Collingwood's primary school. The Red Cross arranged it, and I went with our students. The principal gave an overview of Canada's education system—its structure, values, and goals. Our students joined in volleyball games and recited the English poems they had practiced. It was a beautiful exchange that built bridges and softened fears. I saw light in their eyes that day—glimpses of confidence returning.

As weeks passed, kindness kept showing up. Locals from nearby towns—and even from Toronto—visited often. They brought supplies, but more importantly, they brought themselves. They came to listen, to connect. Some even invited families into their homes. Among them were three Red Cross volunteers. They invited us to spend a day with them in Barrie, about half an hour away. We didn't realize how much we needed it until we got there.

They brought us to a peaceful lake, the kind untouched by sorrow. We had a picnic, laughed, ate slowly, and let ourselves breathe. As a surprise, they arranged a boat ride across the water. I remember the gentle rocking of the boat, the breeze on my face, and the shimmering lake beneath the setting sun. For the first time in a long while, I felt light again. That boat didn't just carry us across water—it lifted us, if only briefly, from the weight we'd been carrying.

A few days later, a school volunteer invited my family into her home. That simple act opened doors. Two more Toronto families welcomed us for overnight stays. One of them, a writer for a children's magazine, had recently published a story for Kosovar children. Her gesture wasn't just hospitality—it was a connection. Through these small but powerful acts of care, we began to feel something we hadn't felt in a long time: a sense of belonging. Even far from home, surrounded by uncertainty, strangers became friends. Their compassion helped us begin the slow, delicate process of healing.

Decisions and Dilemmas

In early July 1999, clerks began interviewing refugees to determine their preferred cities for resettlement. For many of us, the idea of returning to Kosovo was not just daunting—it was heartbreaking. The country we had fled was now ravaged by war, its future uncertain and haunted by fresh memories of violence. Like many others, I hesitated. Our home had been looted and burned by Serbian security forces. The thought of returning to the charred remains of our past felt unbearable, almost cruel.

At first, I imagined staying abroad for a decade or more, determined to build a safe, stable future for our children. Beneath that resolve, however, was a gnawing worry: Would I have access to proper medical care? Would my health hold up in a fragile system still reeling from the war? The economy was in ruins. Recovery, if it came, would be painfully slow. Still, I held on to hope, quietly telling myself that if things improved, we might one day go back. But for now, that hope lay buried beneath the weight of a decision no one should ever have to make.

The United Nations played a critical role during this time, coordinating the return of 89,000 refugees and arranging flights from over thirty countries. Their efforts reunited families and allowed many to begin again in familiar, if wounded, surroundings.

In Canada, officials strongly encouraged us to stay, aligning with the UN's broader strategy. They urged patience, assuring us we could visit Kosovo before making any final, life-altering decisions. Still, restlessness grew. Some refugees petitioned the UNHCR in Ottawa, pleading to return home sooner, desperate to reclaim some control over their lives.

After our interview, my family submitted our city preference with one clear priority: education. We wanted our children to have access to good universities—an opportunity we had never dared dream of back home. The clerks recommended London, Ontario. They warned jobs might be scarce there, but the city offered promise, and for us, that was enough.

Two weeks later, the camp buzzed with nervous

anticipation. Whispers swirled about a place ominously nicknamed "the town of the white bears"—a phrase that stirred both curiosity and dread. The name eventually surfaced: Thunder Bay, Ontario. A remote northern city, often mistaken for being near the Arctic Circle. Fear swept through the camp like a cold wind. Some refugees were so distressed they refused to go. A senior immigration officer was brought in to calm our fears, assuring us no polar bears roamed its streets.

But reassurance couldn't quiet my dread. My anxiety spiked when I realized our name wasn't on the first posted list. A knot tightened in my chest as I imagined being sent somewhere we hadn't chosen—maybe even to Thunder Bay. I feared our voices might be drowned out by bureaucracy.

At the next refugee meeting, I stood and spoke, my voice trembling but determined, echoing the fear many of us carried.

"Honoured officer," I said, standing in a room thick with tension, "we were promised a stable future in Canada and the freedom to choose our city. My family chose London, Ontario. But our name is missing from the list. I'm afraid we'll be sent to Thunder Bay instead. If that happens, after everything we've endured, we may have no choice but to return to Kosovo. Please—do not take advantage of our vulnerability."

Silence filled the room.

The official said nothing.

The meeting ended, but the silence lingered. I walked away with a heavy heart, gripped by a deep sense of helplessness and isolation in a country still unfamiliar, still foreign.

A Choice to Return to Kosovo

Later, I confided in my wife, Meri, my voice barely a whisper under the weight of uncertainty. The fear of being uprooted again—of returning to a homeland that no longer felt like home—was almost unbearable. I tried to explain: if we were sent to Thunder Bay, there was a real chance we'd be forced to return. The thought consumed me. Could we find stability in yet another unfamiliar place, or were we destined to wander, carrying exile with us wherever we went?

That night, sleep evaded me. My mind spiralled with worries—our future, our safety, our health. Morning came, but the rest did not. I forced down a few bites of breakfast, each one a struggle. Exhaustion clouded my thoughts as I stumbled to school, barely able to return the concerned glances of the refugees I passed. My body moved, but I felt detached, like I was watching someone else go through the motions. At the office, Kabashi took one look at me and frowned.

"What's the matter, Mamil? You look exhausted," he said gently.

"I didn't sleep," I said, my voice raw. "If they move me to Thunder Bay, I might have to return to Kosovo. I hoped we could finally settle here. But every time we start to build something, it's torn away."

"Don't make any quick decisions," he said, placing a reassuring hand on my shoulder. "Let me talk to Heidi. She needs to hear this."

Heidi oversaw both the school and the Red Cross. She was always courteous, though I wasn't sure how much power she had. Still, Kabashi's concern gave me the strength to return to class. I made it through the first lesson wearing a mask of calm that felt paper-thin. Later, I stopped by the office to drop off a student's notebook. The school noise buzzed in my ears—too loud, too much. I stepped outside, desperate for stillness. Heidi found me there. Her expression was solemn, but her eyes held something more—resolve.

"I won't let you return to Kosovo," she said, her voice steady. "I'll speak to immigration. We'll get your case reviewed again."

Her words were a lifeline. A flicker of hope in the fog. I nearly broke down, but held it together. I wiped my eyes, nodded, and returned to class. That afternoon, exhaustion overtook me. For two hours, I slept deeply, dreamlessly— untethered from pain, fear, and uncertainty.

Shifting Destinations

Meanwhile, Meri and the children had joined the rest of the family at the camp park. While I slept, unaware, an immigration official came by, knocking several times. I heard nothing. Eventually, he entered and gently called my name. I woke, disoriented, to find him standing beside me, holding a sealed envelope. "I'm sorry to wake you," he said softly.

Still groggy, I stumbled to the bathroom, splashed cold water on my face, and tried to clear my thoughts. With trembling hands, I opened the envelope. I found my name, my family's names, and our relocation city among the documents. My heart sank. It was the same town I had already refused. Panic surged. I rushed to find Meri, needing to confirm what I feared. We met beneath our usual oak tree—the one constant in a world that kept shifting. There, I tore the envelope open again, desperate for clarity. This time, I froze. One word leapt from the page: *London*. Not the rejected town. London. I stared, stunned.

What I hadn't known was that Heidi had written a heartfelt letter to immigration on our behalf. She spoke of our children, our longing for stability, and our willingness to work hard for a better life.

The envelope held more details about a new apartment, names of local sponsors, and a welcome kit with essentials. It felt like a miracle. A door we thought shut had quietly opened. But even in that moment of relief, a shadow remained. Meri's mother, sister, brother, and his young family hadn't been listed for relocation. Their future was still uncertain. The joy of a fresh start was burdened by the fear we might never be reunited. And through it all, the thought of returning to Kosovo—of what that might mean—never fully left my mind.

Moving to an Unknown Town

Two days later, we were ready to board the bus to London, Ontario. The camp courtyard filled with refugees—faces etched with sorrow and fragile hope. They were saying goodbye to forty members of our community, all bound for the same unfamiliar town. Some stood in silence; others wept quietly—grappling with the ache of separation and the uncertainty of what lay ahead.

The camp, once a place of hardship, had become a sanctuary of resilience and shared struggle. Leaving it felt like both a blessing and a heartbreak—a severing of bonds forged in adversity. As we embraced and exchanged farewells, many still clung to the dream of returning to Kosovo, while others braced for a journey to cities they'd only heard about in whispers.

Meri and the children were tearful as they parted from the rest of the family. The weight of that moment was unbearable. These ties—born of loss, survival, and love—had become lifelines. In silent prayer, we wished for reunion, for healing, for the day this separation would become only a memory. After final checks of the refugee lists, the bus pulled away from the military base that had been our home for three months. It felt like an unspoken promise—that even in distance; we remained connected. With every passing mile, we moved farther from the past and deeper into a future we could not yet see.

The three-hour journey blurred past unfamiliar landscapes. A quiet current of fear and anticipation ran through the bus. When we reached London, the city swallowed us in its rhythm, noise, and size. At the reception point, immigration clerks, sponsors, and members of the press greeted us. Some said, "You're safe now." Others offered handshakes and warm smiles. Their presence was a quiet assurance—a small light at the edge of a new beginning.

The government had arranged for each family to be supported by five volunteers over the next two years. These sponsors became our lifeline—helping with errands, daily tasks, and emotional support. They guided us to modest, government-rented flats. Though plain, they felt like a foothold toward rebuilding. Every room held both relief and the quiet ache of what we had left behind.

In the days that followed, we focused on the practicalities

of starting over: enrolling children in school, opening bank accounts, navigating unfamiliar systems. Language barriers made every task more difficult. I began interpreting for fellow refugees—helping them through the maze of bureaucracy. It gave me purpose—a way to ease not just my burden, but theirs.

A week later, we heard from Meri's family. They had decided to return to Kosovo. The news struck like a blow. For Meri, it was especially painful—her mother, brother, sister, and their children had been her emotional foundation. Now they were gone—their names on a different list: UNHCR's, for returnees. The distance between them was no longer just physical. It marked the beginning of a painful reshaping of the family.

Meanwhile, I continued volunteering, and our circle of support grew. Meri's cousin, for example, was embraced by fifteen volunteers from St. Anne's Anglican Church. Their care mirrored the kindness we'd received—a reminder of the shared humanity that bridged faith and background.

Soon after we settled into our flat, Heidi, the head of the local Red Cross, visited us with the English teacher from the Borden base. A month later, the primary school teacher from Collingwood came to check in. Their visits felt like echoes from our recent past—a thread tying our old life to this new one.

They asked how we were adjusting, how the children were doing, whether we felt even a little at home. Their presence lifted our spirits. But after they left, the quiet returned—and with it, the weight of the unknown. Though we had shelter and support, the ache of dislocation remained.

Our days grew heavier, our thoughts often drifting to what we had lost—and to the uncertain road still ahead.

A Return to Kosovo

Exactly one year after arriving in Canada as a refugee, I was granted permission to return to Kosovo. Immigration policies had shifted, and though I still lacked a passport, I received a travel document. Refugees are typically barred from returning to their home countries for five years, but Kosovars were given special exception. The process moved faster than I'd expected, and by early May 2000, I was on a flight back—my heart heavy with both anticipation and dread.

My parents, two sisters, and niece had returned shortly after the war ended in June 1999, aided by volunteers from Tetova. Our original home had been destroyed; the new one ravaged by fire. They found temporary shelter in a small outbuilding in Ferizaj, sleeping on cold, damp earth inside makeshift huts. The house itself was grim—wet, musty, and steeped in the stench of decay.

The morning after I arrived, I walked to what remained of our family home. I stood frozen, staring at the wreckage—the old house and cattle shed reduced to rubble, the new house blackened and unrecognizable. Two rooms and the corridor were completely burned; wiring stripped and destroyed. On the scorched walls, Serbian military graffiti remained—emblems of their flag and the ominous Cyrillic "C"s—a chilling mark of their presence. Even the place where I had hidden our photographs, documents, and keepsakes had been ransacked. Nothing had been spared.

Earlier that year, the German humanitarian group Cap

Anamur began providing aid to rebuild homes. With their support—and our savings for materials and labour—we rebuilt the house in a month. It wasn't perfect, but it stood. It was home again. My parents could finally return to Firajë—to their land, their history—a quiet, powerful reclaiming of life from the ruins.

After a month in Kosovo, I returned to Canada, carrying the weight of all I had seen. But beneath the sorrow, something else stirred—a glimmer of resilience, a quiet hope. The healing had begun, however slowly. And for the first time, I believed we might find our way back.

Disappointment to Delight

After returning from Kosovo, time stretched endlessly; each day steeped in quiet sorrow for what lay ahead. We had hoped that, after a decade, things would improve—that our sacrifices, patience, and resilience would finally bear fruit. But the roots of war ran deep, and Serbia's ongoing threats cast a long shadow over any progress. The region's future felt as fragile as ever. Economic growth had stalled, unemployment was painfully high, healthcare was crumbling, and the education system offered little promise. Going back to my hometown became not just difficult, but impossible.

Gradually, the dream of return faded. Canada—once a temporary refuge—had become our permanent home. With heavy hearts but quiet resolve, we accepted this new land as our foundation. Yet even as we moved forward, we carried the ache of a homeland out of reach—a place we still loved, even as it slipped further away.

But time, with its quiet patience, softened the weight of

disappointment. Though the dream of return never fully left us, a different life slowly unfolded here. Canada, once a place of refuge, became our home. Three of our children married and built their lives in this country, raising seven children of their own—some now in primary school, one in high school, and others still growing, filling our days with laughter and energy. One of them has just begun their first year at Western University, and I still remember the pride in their eyes—and the tears in mine—as we stood together on campus for the first time. Our second daughter settled in Germany, where she lives with her husband and their three children—carrying forward another branch of our family's journey. Between them all, Meri and I are now blessed with ten grandchildren.

I am retired now. My days are quieter, shaped by familiar routines—walking, reading, writing, and the joy of watching our grandchildren grow.

Meri and I often reflect on the road behind us, grateful for the safety and peace that this country has offered us. The ache of exile still lingers, but so does the quiet strength of a life rebuilt with dignity. The longing for our homeland will never leave us, but here, surrounded by family and memory, we have found a measure of peace. Life, in many ways, has turned out all right.

Fatmir Sadiku, human rights activist, was born in Firajë, Kosovo and graduated from the College of Belgrade in Hospitality Services/Administration. He was a journalist at Rilindja *daily newspaper and worked as a high school teacher for thirteen years. He moved to Canada with his wife and five children in May 1999.*

HEAVENS TO MURGATROYD
stories & poems

A fun collection of diverse stories and poems that *The Ottawa Review of Books* observes, "ranges from poetry to psychology, from genre to character study, from light to serious." Each piece features a character called Murgatroyd.

Contributors include Finnian Burnett, Zilla Jones, Robert Runté, Renee Cronley, Trent Lewin, Laurène Boutin, M. Gail Stelter, Donnalyn Rainey, Lindsay Harrington, T.L. Tomljanovic, Alma Lee, Lavinia Leon, Tom McCann, Robyn Diner, Shawn L. Bird, Trevor Hodges, Susan Duffield Lodge, Sherry Cassells and Janet Richards.

PLATYPUS TALES
Short stories celebrating the oddly unexpected

A quartet of stories celebrating the delightfully odd, from Finnian Burnett, Chris McMahen, Shawn L. Bird, and Janet Whitehead.

GHOSTLY

13 tales from beyond the veil

A collection of haunting short stories from Alix Kelinda, Finnian Burnett, Halli Reid, Jarrod K Williams, Jeanna Mason Stay, Kaitlyn Petry, L. N. Hunter, Lee F. Patrick, Leslie Wibberley, Marie Powell, Rob Nisbet, Shawn L. Bird, and Theric Jepson.

THE DRAGON PROBLEM
a collaborative novel

The village of Zos has a dragon problem.
Follow the townsfolk as they deal with an evil dentist, a decrepit
dragon, a musical milkmaid, and political shenanigans.

A roomful of authors brainstormed this novel at When Words
Collide Writers' Conference in 2023 and 10 authors worked
together in subsequent months to craft this entertaining tale.

NEW SPACES:
an anthology of sci-fi short stories

Within your mind and across the universe, there are new spaces to explore!

From Lintusen Press comes this collection of ten science fiction short stories from authors Finnian Burnett, Andrew G. Cooper, J. Paul Cooper, BC Deeks, Nancy Kilpatrick, Philip Mann, Lee F. Patrick, Halli Reid, KT Wagner, and Jarrod K. Williams.

SMALL SHIFTS:
short stories of fantastical transformation

Not all shifters turn into magnificent beasts. Sure, there are those humans who transform into wolves and bears, but this book is about the smaller creatures. Learn about the trials and tribulations of folks who turn into raccoons, hamsters, mosquitoes, or bumblebees. 11 delightful tales of Small Shifts.

THE DRABBLE ADVENT CALENDAR

A drabble is a story of precisely one hundred words. Here are 25 family friendly winter themed drabbles; one perfectly complete tidbit of story to savour each day leading up to Christmas from authors Carol Parchewsky, Chris McMahen, Finnian Burnett, Lee F. Patrick, Shawn L. Bird, and Tim Reynolds.

Please visit

LintusenPress.ca

to learn more about our upcoming releases
and to see submission calls
for our future publications.

Thank you for leaving a review

on your favourite site or retailer
if you enjoyed this book.